in Circus Quirkus

Erin Soderberg

Illustrated by Kelly Light

BLOOMSBURY

LONDON NEW DELHI NEW YORK SYDNEY

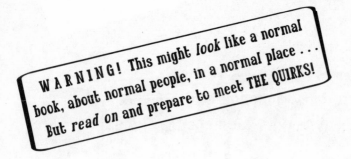

WARNING! This might *look* like a normal book, about normal people, in a normal place . . . But *read on* and prepare to meet THE QUIRKS!

Bloomsbury Publishing, London, New Delhi, New York and Sydney

First published in Great Britain in February 2014 by Bloomsbury Publishing Plc
50 Bedford Square, London WC1B 3DP

First published in the USA in February 2014 by Bloomsbury Publishing Plc
1385 Broadway, New York, New York 10018

A CIP catalogue record for this book is available from the British Library

ISBN 978 1 4088 4293 5

MIX
Paper from
responsible sources
FSC® C020471
www.fsc.org

1 3 5 7 9 10 8 6 4 2

Printed and bound in Great Britain by CPI Group (UK) Ltd, Croydon CR0 4YY

www.bloomsbury.com

For the students and teachers at
Burroughs Elementary School
—E. S.

To Meghan and Cate,
two wonderfully quirky girls!
—K. L.

Table of Contents

CHAPTER 1

Sticky, Hairy Secrets

All families have secrets. Some keep itty-bitty secrets. Others hold sad and heavy secrets. Many have funny-looking secrets that they try to hide beneath shirts or under caps or in tucked-away attic eaves.

A few families, however, keep more than their fair share of secrets: big, hairy monsters who love long naps on the couch. Grandmothers so small they can fit into the palm of your hand. Brothers who disappear with the sticky *pop* of a bubble. A sister whose mind has a mind of its own.

The Quirks were one of these families. They had huger, hairier, twistier and stickier secrets than any other family on their block. No one knew it yet – because the Quirk family worked hard to hide the things that set them apart from the ordinary. Some days, their differences were a good thing; some days, they were not. But *every* day, this was a family that went to great lengths to try to fit in. They kept their business tucked behind tall fences and hoped no one would notice that goings-on at the Quirk house were more peculiar than most people might expect.

But as it happens, someone *had* taken notice. This someone had started to figure out that strange things were afoot in the perfectly ordinary town of Normal, Michigan.

And that is where we begin.

CHAPTER 2

strange Neighbours

"Molly!" Five-year-old Finnegan Quirk lifted his hands in the air and jumped up and down. "I'm open! Pass it wide."

Molly Quirk twisted a football in her hand. Then she let it sail into the garden. Molly watched as her younger brother leaped into the air and caught the ball between his grimy palms. A perfect shot. "Yes!" she cried, clapping. "Nice catch, Finn!"

Finn shimmied and did a celebration dance. He waved the football from side to side in front of his body, dancing like a professional American football player after the game-winning touchdown. He threw the ball into the air, then caught it and danced with it again. As he danced, he taunted in a sing-song voice, "I rule, I caught the ball, I rule, I caught the ball . . . *OOF!*"

Suddenly, Finn was on his back and the football spun in the grass beside him.

"Tackle!" Penelope Quirk whooped, pinning her little brother's body to the grass. She tickled him until he shrieked from the torture and stopped squirming. Penelope pumped her fist in the air and looked up at Molly, who was watching her twin sister and Finn wrestle from the safety of the back deck.

"How did you find him to tackle him?" Molly asked, leaning over the edge of the deck rail. Her long, dark, crinkly curls sprung out from her head as if they wanted to join in the game, too.

Penelope beamed. Her expression matched her twin sister's exactly, even down to a slightly raised left eyebrow. "If Finn hadn't been waving the football in the air, I never *would* have found him. Your boastful little dance gave you away, Finn! You should have hidden the ball in your shirt and run instead of gloating. Then you would have made it to the fence and scored, no problem."

"Not fair." Finn sulked, wedging his body out of his sister's tackle hold. He plopped down on the grass with his arms wrapped around his legs. He buried his face between his thighs. His wild mop of blonde hair stuck straight up, making it look like his bony knees had grown a full head of hair. Molly giggled at the sight of it.

"Not fair?" Penelope huffed, grabbing the football off the grass. As she tossed it from hand to hand, the ball turned bright pink with green polka dots. "You think this game isn't fair for *you*? You're *invisible*, Finn – and I'm stuck trying to tackle you! Do you know how hard that is?"

Molly laughed even harder. Games of any kind were tricky in the Quirk house. When you live with a family of magical misfits, regular daily things like tossing around a ball were anything but ordinary. Molly Quirk knew this better than anyone. She was plain and magic-less, the only Quirk

without a "Quirk", but the rest of her family was definitely *not*.

Molly's little brother, Finn, was invisible – unless he was chewing gum.

Her twin sister, Penelope, had a super-amazing magical imagination that made some of the ideas in her head come to life in an uncontrollable *poof!* (Or a *plop!*, if you count the time Penelope had made a toilet submarine appear in the girls' bathroom at school.)

Her mother, Bree, could make people believe just about anything she told them to believe (and she could also make people do stinky things they didn't want to do, like wipe up the bathroom floor).

Her grandfather Quilliam Quirk was able to twist and rewind time. His magic worked like the Back button on a DVR remote.

And Molly's gran . . . well, she was as tiny as a bird.

Even though Molly didn't have any secret talents or hidden magic, there *were* things that made her special: she was immune to much of her family's magic. She was the only person on earth who could see her brother when he wasn't chewing gum. She could never be mind-controlled by her mum. She always knew – and *felt* – when her grandpa Quill was twisting time. And though Gran was still tiny, even to Molly's eyes, Molly could hear her grandmother much better than anyone else in the family could. But even Molly wasn't immune to her sister's magic. They had a feeling that was a twin thing.

The Quirk family was certainly different. They had their secrets. But that was OK. Because sometimes, Molly knew, being a little bit different was just fine – especially when you could keep those differences hidden.

"Can I play?" Grandpa Quill muttered sleepily from the corner of the deck. He'd been relaxing in a broken-down Adirondack chair for most of the morning, dozing as his grandchildren played football in the garden. Grandpa often needed a nap after a big meal, or after he'd used his magic too many times. Today, his sleepiness was the direct result of six or seven too many pancakes at breakfast.

Gran, who spent much of her time hiding away inside her itty-bitty house that hung from a tucked-away branch in the willow tree, sat on the arm of his chair. She was busy knitting tiny little jumpers to wrap around her tomatoes. The first overnight frost wasn't too far off, and she'd decided to try something new to keep them from freezing during a chilly spell.

Grandpa Quill stood up and stretched. "I'll just go get my jerseys. Then we can play a proper game of American football." He returned a few minutes later. His arms were stuffed with at least a dozen colourful football jerseys, all with different team logos.

"Let's see," he said, surveying the pile of jerseys

he'd dumped on the deck. "Should I play for the Rams or the Packers? Ooh – the Giants? Eagles?" Grandpa held up a rainbow of jerseys, one after another. "The Eagles' green makes me think of Scotland's rolling hills and those sweet, stinky, hairy cows. Bless the Homeland." He kissed the jersey, then slipped it on over his white T-shirt and braces.

Gran shook her tiny head. "Scotland," she squeaked. "Second only to my fair Ireland. Am I right, Quilliam?"

"Ireland is certainly nice, dear," Grandpa Quill said. "But Scotland is far superior. We have haggis." This was a playful argument Gran and Grandpa Quirk had been having for as long as Molly could remember. She'd never been to Ireland *or* Scotland, but they both looked pretty in all her grandparents' pictures (haggis, however, was a disgusting Scottish sausage thing that was stuffed inside an animal *stomach* – ew!). Anyway, Molly reasoned, they lived in America now, so she didn't really get why it mattered. For the Quirks, who were always moving, home was much more about people than place – at least, that's what their mum had always said.

"How many jerseys do you have, Gramps?" Finn asked, coming over for a closer look. He pawed through the pile, practising his counting. When he got to nine, Finn popped a gumball out of his pocket and into his mouth. In the next instant, his body shivered into view.

Grandpa Quill blinked at his grandson. Finn had only recently figured out the gum trick. So it was still a little unsettling when he went from *invisible* to *visible* with a quick chomp on his gum.

"I've got more than a dozen," Grandpa replied. The Eagles jersey fit snugly against his ample belly, so he tugged on it to try to give his stomach some room to relax. "I like to get a jersey from every place we live. Shows my hometown spirit."

"Shouldn't you have twenty-six jerseys, then?" Penelope asked. Pen knew, better than anyone else in the family, just how many towns the Quirks had lived in during the nine (and three-quarters) years she and Molly had been alive. "One for each place we've lived?"

Grandpa stroked his long, white moustache. "Yep, Normal is town number twenty-seven. But some states we've lived in don't have a football team, so I just get a souvenir T-shirt from those places instead. That's how I ended up with my 'Honk If You Like Pickles' shirt." He cleared his throat. "Ah, that's a good one. I do love pickles." He chuckled, then pawed through the pile of jerseys again. "Twenty-seven towns in the last ten years, can you believe it? Let's hope there isn't a number twenty-eight."

The Quirk family moved around a lot. Sometimes, as soon as they'd get settled in a town, they would have to move again. They'd open their boxes of stuff, then quickly tape them back up. Every time they had to move, it was because someone's magic had got the family in trouble with a capital Q. But now they had made themselves at home in Normal, Michigan, and every last one of the Quirks wanted to stay for good. Molly knew that would only be possible if they could keep the family's secrets hush-hush.

Grandpa Quill plucked a jersey from the pile for Finn to wear. Then he dug through the stack to find one for Molly and one for Penelope. Penelope crinkled her nose at the ugly maroon jersey he dropped in her hands. Grandpa surveyed the rest of the stack and said, "This reminds me that I've still got to get myself a Detroit Lions jersey."

As Molly slipped a Chicago Bears jersey over her clothes, she suddenly got a strange feeling that someone was watching her. She looked around, feeling goose bumps prickle under her skin as the sensation of being watched grew and grew. Finally, her eyes settled on the round, egg-size hole in the tall fence between the Quirks' garden and their neighbour's garden. An eyeball was peering through that hole, watching them.

"Mrs DeVille," Molly whispered, quietly enough that no one else could hear. The Quirks' neighbour on the left wasn't a bad lady, but she *was* cranky. Molly and Penelope sometimes joked that it almost seemed like she was allergic to kids. In the few short weeks the Quirks had lived next to her, they'd got the distinct impression that she *really* didn't like Molly, Pen or Finn. She made Molly especially nervous after what had happened late the night before.

The Quirks had come home from a big night of sticky, record-setting fun at Normal Night, their new town's annual festival. When they opened their fence gate, they had found a surprise waiting for them: Mrs DeVille was *on* their front porch. As the Quirks stumbled up their crumbly front steps, they caught her standing tippy-toed on her stubby feet, peeking into their house!

Fortunately, Bree Quirk used her magic to convince Mrs DeVille to go home, and to forget whatever it was she had seen. But now Mrs DeVille was snooping on them again . . . and snoops made Molly uneasy.

Molly knew it was one thing to try to keep their magic hidden when they were out – at school, or at Crazy Ed's restaurant, or with their friends. But it was another thing altogether for the Quirks to have to keep their magic under lock and key at *home*, too. There had to be somewhere that they could just be themselves!

Molly pulled the football jersey down until it hung past her knobbly knees like a dress. Then she glared back at Mrs DeVille, silently wishing their neighbour would just mind her own business already. But as hard as Molly stared, Mrs DeVille stared back even harder.

Really, it was quite lucky that Mrs DeVille was so focused on winning her staring contest with Molly. Because if she'd shifted her attention just twenty-four inches to the right, she would have seen Finn going from visible to invisible in the blink of an eye.

CHAPTER 3

Threat Throwdown

Molly cOntinued to stare at Mrs DeVille until her neighbour's big, bulgy eyeball blinked and disappeared from view.

A moment later, Bree Quirk breezed on to the deck, wearing her apron with the dancing chickens on it. "I'm home," she sang sweetly. Bree was a waitress at Crazy Ed's, a diner-style restaurant on Old County Road Six. "Breakfast at Ed's was nutty this morning. It seems no one wanted to cook after Normal Night." She collapsed into a chair and patted at her crazy flyaway hair.

When Bree used too much of her magic – something she often had to do while she was at work, since she was a terrible waitress – she would start to feel faint and dizzy. She'd come home looking like she'd gone through the spin cycle on the washing machine. "Today was a killer," she said, closing her eyes to rest.

Out in the garden, Finn and Grandpa Quill were now playing dodge ball. Finn kept cheating by taking his gum out of his mouth and going invisible, but Grandpa didn't seem to mind. Gran had gotten into the game, too. She chased after the ball and whacked it with her knitting needle whenever it sailed too close to her herb garden.

"Do you want something to drink, Mum?" Penelope asked. Then she squeezed her eyes closed, balled her hands into fists and focused. Through clenched teeth, she muttered, "I can get you something if you want."

Suddenly, a glass with one inch of dirty-looking water appeared out of nowhere. A fly buzzed by and landed in it. As Penelope stared at the water, the fly began to do the backstroke. The nearly empty glass teetered and tottered on the arm of Bree's chair, then fell to the ground and shattered. The fly buzzed away.

Penelope opened her eyes and sighed. "I tried." She shrugged. "Maybe I should just get you a glass of water the normal way."

"That might be a good idea," Bree agreed. She patted Penelope on the arm. "I'll get this mess cleaned up." She closed her eyes and tipped her head so the sun shone on her face. "In a minute."

Pen headed inside, grumbling to herself. Ever since she was a baby, Penelope Quirk's mind had worked differently. Like other fourth graders, Pen's head was stuffed full of ideas and imagination. But unlike other kids, when she was distracted or nervous or super-extra-uncomfortable, the silly thoughts in her head would – *poof!* – come to life. Lately she and Molly had noticed that Pen's Quirk popped up more when things were especially crazy around them.

Usually, whatever Penelope's mind cooked up

would disappear in a matter of moments. Gymnasiums full of butterflies or polka-dotted fish or milk cartons that danced around on tiny little legs would usually fade into mist within seconds. But sometimes, the secret bits of Penelope's mind would stick around and make themselves at home – like Pen's pet monster, Niblet. Sweet, scaredy-cat Niblet had been a part of the Quirk family for the past few years, and no one quite knew why.

Ever since she'd realised just how different she was, Penelope had been trying to figure out how to control her Quirk. She didn't like that her magic sometimes got her family in trouble, and she hated that she couldn't control her own head. In the last few weeks, Pen had discovered that if there was something she wanted really badly – and she focused her whole mind and body on making it happen – her mind would maybe, possibly, do what she told it to do. But like everything with Pen's Quirk, there were no guarantees. Even still, she'd been practising. And practising. And practising some more.

Penelope returned from the kitchen with a

full glass of clear, cold water. She made a wide arc around the chunks of broken glass and placed the water on the wooden deck beside Bree's feet. "Here, Mum. Sorry about the broken glass." Pen looked ashamed.

"It's not a big deal, sweetheart," Bree said, her eyes still closed. "I understand that you need to practise."

Molly suddenly got the feeling of being watched again. She snuck a peek at the hole in the fence. Sure enough, Mrs DeVille was back. And this time, she was wearing her glasses.

"Mum," Molly whispered urgently. "Mrs DeVille is spying on us again."

"I'm sure she's just gardening," Bree murmured. Her eyes were still closed, and there was a small smile on her face. "It's a beautiful autumn day, so a lot of people are outside."

"No, Mum," Molly said, poking her mother in the foot. She pointed at Mrs DeVille. "Look."

Bree opened her eyes and followed the line of Molly's finger. "Well, what do you know?" Bree lifted one hand and waved. "Let's just be friendly. I'm sure everything's fine." But Bree did not sound convinced. Her voice was shaky, and her eyebrows were pulled together in a not-fine sort of way.

Mrs DeVille didn't wave back. Her eye blinked behind the hole in the fence, then she went on staring.

"I wonder what she's so curious about?" Bree wondered.

Molly's mouth hung open. She whispered, "You *wonder what she's so curious about?*" Her gaze flickered to the garden, where Grandpa Quill was running around screeching. He was still wearing his silly, too-tight football jersey while he leaped and jumped around like a dog chasing a butterfly. Since Finn was invisible, it looked like Grandpa was dodging madly around the garden blabbering to himself. Every once in a while, Finn would whoop with joy, his voice coming out of nowhere. Gran buzzed around them, swatting at the ball like some sort of angry bird. Meanwhile, Penelope's football jersey kept switching from pink to green and then back to maroon again. The whole scene was really odd and very curious.

"Good afternoon, Mrs DeVille," Bree cooed

sweetly. "I hope you had a restful night!"

Mrs DeVille grunted in response. "What kind of shirt is that, anyway?" she asked after a moment. She looked at Penelope and blinked. "I've never seen a shirt do that before. Not a normal shirt, anyway."

Pen glanced down and gasped. She crouched and tried to cover the colour-changing jersey with her arms and legs. As Penelope panicked, the colours began to shift quicker and quicker, until her shirt swirled into a rainbow of ever-changing colours.

"It's just a football jersey, Mrs DeVille," Bree said, sitting up straighter. She tried to make eye contact with Mrs DeVille, but Mrs DeVille was distracted, her eye looking this way and that. Molly could sense her mother's Quirk getting ready for action. Bree's power – the ability to make people think or do things – was very limited. Her magic could only stretch as far as two, maybe three, people at a time. And she had to look them straight in the eye for her powers to work right. "That's a normal football jersey," she said, focusing on Mrs DeVille.

Bree stood up and made her way towards the tall fence. Finn and Grandpa Quill stopped playing their game to see what was happening. Finn hid in the corner of the garden. He slipped the piece of gum out from behind his ear and into his mouth. Then he came back into view. Bree put her eye up close to the hole in the fence and fixed her gaze on Mrs DeVille. "Nothing to see over here, Mrs DeVille. There is nothing interesting for you to see."

"I get that there's nothing to see," Mrs DeVille said crossly. "But that doesn't mean I don't think you folks are odd. And I don't like secrets." She backed away from the fence. "I bet you've got something to hide over there. I've been watching you."

"You haven't been watching us, Mrs DeVille," Bree said, her voice steady. She waited until Mrs DeVille met her gaze to continue. "You need to believe me when I say we have nothing to hide. You can just mind your own business now, dear, and forget what you've just seen through the hole in the fence."

Mrs DeVille looked convinced for a moment. But then she narrowed her eye again, as though she'd just remembered something. "I don't know why I can't stop looking at you people." She blinked. "But if I see any funny business, I'm calling the police!"

She stepped back from the hole in the fence, but her voice rang out clear when she said, "Or I'll call the news reporters! Don't care who, but I'll talk to whoever will listen. I will figure out what secrets you're hiding over there . . . and I'll make sure the rest of this town finds out, too!"

CHAPTER 4

Swinging
Surprise

"Ladies and gently-men!" Molly and Penelope's fourth-grade teacher, Mr Intihar, clapped his big hands to call attention. "Folks! Settle down and line up. We're due in the gym in three minutes."

Molly and Penelope stepped into line with the rest of their class. Today, Normal Elementary School was having its very first assembly of the school year. The rumour among the students was that there was going to be a big announcement of some kind. Big announcements were always super-fun.

Penelope Quirk may have been the only fourth grader who felt not so good. She'd been feeling sort of icky all weekend, and there were two possible explanations for it. One was that she'd eaten *way* too much sugar at Normal Night (she'd had candy floss, a paper cone full of chocolate chip cookies, and a whole lot of gum). The other, more likely, possibility was that Mrs DeVille's snooping had set her nerves on edge.

"Nolan! Raade! Joey! That's enough . . . Please fall into line." Mr Intihar ran his hand through his shock of fluffy hair and began to count the students in line. As he did, Nolan Paulson and Joey Pahula both stumbled and fell into the line of kids. They knocked into Raade Gears, and all three boys fell over in a heap. At first, Nolan and Joey looked surprised – but then they cracked up laughing.

Molly nudged her sister. Penelope closed her eyes and began to hum, trying to distract herself from her thoughts. Her mind had taken Mr Intihar's command very literally. Luckily, everyone else in the class was so busy laughing about Nolan and Joey actually *falling* into the line that they didn't pay Penelope and her imagination any mind.

As the fourth-grade class followed Mr Intihar down the curved hallway to the gym entrance, they passed the kindergartners lining up outside Mrs Risdall's classroom. Molly waved at Finn. Her brother stuck out his tongue, which was covered in a thick layer of bubble gum. Finn was always supposed to chew gum at school. But sometimes, he slipped his gum out of his mouth and sneaked around the school making mischief. He wasn't *supposed* to go invisible at school, but Finn was terrible about following rules.

When they got to the school's huge gym, everyone in the fourth-grade class stopped and stared. The Normal Elementary School gym was enormous, with high, beamed ceilings. But today it felt tiny – because there was a giant trapeze rig set up in the centre of the gym. A big net was strung between two tall posts, and a flying trapeze bar looped down, just waiting for someone to swing on it. "What's with the trapeze?" Stella Anderson asked, leaning into Molly.

"I don't know," Molly answered. She and the rest of the fourth graders found a spot on the floor and tried to settle down.

"Maybe the teachers are going to do some sort of skit!" Another fourth grader, Amelia, kneeled for a better view. The little kids got to sit up front, really close to the trapeze net, but they were already having a hard time sitting still.

Once every class had arrived and the kindergartners sat cross-legged on the floor, the lights in the gym dimmed. Bright, neon spotlights zoomed around the room. Music piped out of speakers up near the trapeze stands. Suddenly, an echoing voice boomed out of the speakers, "Are you ready for the incredible, death-defying stunts of Circus of the Dazzling Stars?"

Everyone cheered.

"I can't hear you!" The voice rumbled with energy. "I *said*, are you ready for Circus of the Dazzling Stars?"

"We are!" Molly and Penelope yelled. The rest

of the school was screaming and shouting, too. "I can't believe this!" Molly leaned in close to speak into Penelope's ear. "A real circus, right here in our own school?"

Pen grinned back, then turned her eyes up front.

"Well, then . . ." The voice cut out suddenly, and the regular fluorescent gym lights flickered on. The neon stopped swirling. Everyone watched as Mr Intihar climbed a skinny rope ladder on to one of the tall trapeze posts and waved. He held up a microphone and – in the same crazy announcer voice – said, "Then start stretching and lace up your gym shoes, because you have work to do first."

Everyone in the gym groaned.

"Now, now," Mr Intihar said, clasping the trapeze bar in one of his enormous hands. "Yes, the Circus of the Dazzling Stars *will* be performing for all of you – right here in the Normal Elementary School gym. But not today. First, we have a special surprise planned." His voice had gone back to normal, and now it just sounded loud and sort of squeaky, like microphone voices often do.

"Swing, Mr I!" Nolan Paulson interrupted from his seat on the gym floor. "Let's see you trapeze!"

Mr Intihar paused, then his eyes scanned over the crowd of students. "What's that? You want to see me trapeze?" he yelled into the microphone. A gargantuan smile spread across his face. He glanced at the school principal, who nodded her approval.

"Yes!" everyone cried.

"You *do?*"

"Yes!" Students were now stomping their feet on the floor and clapping. Some people were chanting, "Mr I! Mr I!"

Mr Intihar reached down from the post and handed the microphone to Mrs Risdall, the kindergarten teacher. She was busy trying to get her students – including Finn – to glue their behinds to the floor.

33

"Well, if you *insist*," Mr Intihar shouted over the noise in the gym. He rubbed his hands through his tufty hair. Then he blew on each of his fingers, curled his hands tight around the trapeze bar, and jumped. His long, lean body swung through the air. His legs dangled from his torso as he swung back and forth. Everyone went wild when Mr Inti-har kicked his legs out in front of him and made the trapeze swing higher and higher.

Finally, with one last pump of his legs, Mr Inti-har let go of the bar and flew upwards. Then he threw his hands out to the sides and landed grace-fully on his back in the net below him.

"That was amazing!" Molly screamed.

"Go, Mr I!" Stella shouted.

Every person in the whole school stood up and cheered. Mr Intihar's body bounced on the net, then he scooted over to the edge and slid down to the floor. He towered over the short little kinder-gartners in the front rows. He bowed, then reached for the microphone again.

When everyone had settled down, he said, "Now, that was pretty cool, wasn't it?"

Everyone clapped and yelled again.

"I've been practising," he boasted. "Who else would like to learn how to fly on the trapeze like a true circus artist?"

Molly and Penelope cheered along with the rest of the school.

Once everyone had quieted down, Nolan stood up and screamed, "I do! I am going to *rock* at trapeze." He lifted his arms in the air and whooped.

"Well, then, I have good news for you." Mr Intihar held up his hand to signal for silence so he could finish his announcement. "Because Circus of the Dazzling Stars will be rehearsing for and performing their show *here*, in *our* gym, Normal Elementary School gets to be involved. The circus folks will be showcasing their incredible acts for everyone in Normal in just two weeks." He paused for dramatic effect. "And the exciting surprise is . . . between now and then, the circus performers will be working with the lot of you during your gym classes so you can learn how to do some of their tricks."

"So cool!" Nolan yelled out.

"Yes, Nolan, it is cool. But perhaps it's time for you to zip those lips and listen," Mr Intihar said into the microphone. He gave Nolan a look that told him he'd better zip it or he'd be sitting on the mats while everyone else swung from the trapeze bar. Penelope giggled, and Molly noticed that

Nolan's lips suddenly seemed like they were fused shut. When Molly leaned over to get a closer look, she realised that they were actually *zipped* closed. Nolan looked sort of panicked, but he'd also finally stopped interrupting.

Mr Intihar nodded at Nolan. "What's even more cool . . ." Their teacher paused. "Is that the students from one lucky and talented class at Normal Elementary School will get to show off what they've learned *onstage* with the circus pros during their performance! One class full of students will showcase the daring, dazzling, death-defying circus stunts you've learned for the whole town of Normal."

"Who?" someone in the fifth grade shouted. "Fifth grade rules!"

"No, kindergartners want to be onstage," a little kindergartener sobbed. "I want to!"

Nolan, for once, said nothing.

"Now, now," Mr Intihar hollered as he tapped the microphone against his head. "There will be a school-wide competition to figure out which of *you* –" he pointed at his audience –

"will get to perform for your friends, families, and neighbours."

"A competition?" Amelia said excitedly from beside Penelope.

"I hope it's a maths competition," Molly added.

Penelope groaned. "I hope it's not."

"This is a skill-based competition. The circus team will determine who the winner is before their performance." Mr Intihar paced back and forth in front of the whole school, waving his wobbly arms around in the air as he talked. His long legs high-stepped over a sprawling kindergartner, and he high-fived Mr Knaus, the first-grade teacher, as he galloped by him. "Vivica and her team of circus pros will be watching you carefully during your lessons in gym class. In two weeks, they will decide which grade is the most ready. You'll all need to pay attention in gym and practise at home – and whoever they feel is most prepared to strut their stuff in the circus ring will win the opportunity to perform in front of the whole town."

Mr Intihar smiled and stopped pacing. He bowed majestically. "And now, you are all dismissed! Just remember – with circus stunts, it's important to keep an open mind and open eyes and believe that anything's possible. If you do that, the prize can be yours."

CHAPTER 5

NuBBly NiBlet

"I want to win so bad," Stella Anderson said excitedly as she, Molly, Penelope and Joey Pahula walked home from school together later that afternoon. It was a beautiful autumn day, the kind that slips in between summer and winter and makes people forget that snow is coming. None of the kids wanted to squeeze into the smelly school bus on such a lovely afternoon, and since they all lived on the same side of town, they'd decided to walk together.

Molly nodded. "I *love* the circus. I can't believe

we actually get to learn how to do some of the circus troupe's tricks. I've always wanted to trapeze."

"Me, too!" Penelope chimed in quietly from a few steps behind Molly and the other kids. Though Molly had started to feel comfortable with some of their classmates and friends after just a few weeks in Normal, Penelope still got nervous. She was often worried her magic would act up, so she sometimes came across as quite shy.

Joey stopped walking to kick at a pile of yellow and brown leaves that someone had raked into a tidy pile in the corner of a garden. They went flying into the air, then rained down in messy clumps around his legs. He blurted out, "I'm kind of a klutz. I hope I don't ruin it for the rest of you."

"None of us are circus pros," Penelope said logically. "You're not the only one who doesn't know what you're doing. And even if we don't win, I'm just so happy we all get to learn circus tricks. Gym class is going to be so cool for the next few weeks."

"I know," Stella agreed. "But don't you want to *win*?"

"And perform in the spotlight in front of the whole town?" Penelope grumbled. "Not really."

Molly slowed down so she could link arms with her sister. "I think it would be really fun to be onstage with the circus people."

Penelope grimaced.

"Well, even if our class doesn't win, at least we get to watch the circus. Nothing cool ever comes to Normal," Stella said. "Other than Normal Night, hardly anything interesting ever happens in this town."

Molly and Penelope shared a look. They knew that plenty of interesting things happened at the Quirks' house – it's just that they kept those things secret. They'd reached the corner of the Quirks' street, so Molly said, "We'll see you guys tomorrow."

Joey and Stella both waved and kept walking towards their own block. "See you guys tomorrow!"

Molly waved, then draped her arm over her

sister's shoulder and marched down the pavement. Once Stella and Joey were out of hearing range, she looked at Penelope. "I saw what you did to Nolan today during the assembly. Zipped his lips up tight."

Penelope giggled. "Yep. I get so sick of him interrupting all the time."

"He does blurt a lot," Molly agreed. "But maybe you should try to ignore him."

"When Nolan gets all wild and boastful and annoying, it's impossible for me to think about or look at anything else." Penelope paused. "It's like that time we saw the smushed squirrel on the street outside our house in Ohio – I kind of didn't want to look, but I couldn't help it."

Molly made a face. "You're saying Nolan is like a smushed squirrel?"

Penelope laughed again. "Yeah. I know I shouldn't pay attention to him, because nothing good will come of it, but I can't help it."

"And then *poof!*" Molly added. "Your magic acts up."

"Yep." Penelope shrugged. Suddenly, she

stopped walking to gaze in the direction of the Quirks' house. "Molly . . . is that Mrs DeVille?"

"What is she doing?" Molly wondered aloud. Mrs DeVille was teetering on a stepladder in her garden. As Molly and Penelope watched, she craned her neck to look over the fence into the Quirks' house. Molly gasped. "I think she's looking in our windows! That's our bedroom window she's trying to peek into, Pen!"

Up in the girls' bedroom, something moved behind the wisp of a curtain. One hairy arm, then a pair of blinking glasses . . . it was Penelope's monster, Niblet! He was staring back at Mrs DeVille!

On her ladder, Mrs DeVille gasped, then uneasily teetered down to a lower step. "What in the . . . ?" She rubbed at her eyes, propped her glasses up on the bridge of her nose, then fixed her gaze on Molly and Penelope's window again. Niblet was no longer there, but Mrs DeVille was still staring.

Penelope chewed at her lip. "She's trying to figure out our secrets again, Mol."

Molly nodded. Both girls knew their snooping neighbour's shenanigans could easily send the Quirks packing. Pen and Molly hustled the rest of the way up the pavement to their front gate. By the time they latched the gate behind themselves and climbed up their crumbling front steps, Mrs DeVille was nowhere to be seen.

"Hello?" Pen called out into the quiet front hall of the Quirks' house. "Anyone home?"

Molly found a note on the dining-room table. "Gramps and Finn went to the shop for rope," she said, pulling her eyebrows together. "Why rope?" A moment later she yelled, "Niblet?"

Pen thundered up the stairs. Molly kicked off her shoes and followed. Niblet usually spent much of his day napping under Penelope's bottom bunk. He liked to stay as close to Pen as possible. Since it was her imagination that brought him to life, he adored her.

"Hey, buddy," Penelope crooned, poking her head around the girls' bedroom door.

The monster popped his head out from under the bed and squeaked in response.

"How was your day?" Pen crouched down on the floor, and Niblet wiggled over to nuzzle his nubbly head against her cheek. Molly tickled the monster's super-teeny toes – she loved hearing his goofy giggle. Niblet curled up on the rug in the centre of the twins' bedroom and looked at them expectantly.

Molly told their monster all about the assembly and about how the circus was coming to town. Niblet loved hearing the girls' stories and *really* loved it when they included him in some way. "We'll teach you some of the stuff we learn, OK?"

Niblet nodded eagerly. Then he scratched his belly and stood up. He giggled as he squeezed his furry body into one of Penelope's tutus and balanced his itty-bitty feet in the centre of a chair to perform a silly mime routine. He sashayed around the room, hopping and waving his arms in the air. He looked more like a prima ballerina than a mime or a clown, but it really didn't matter. Their monster was hilarious and adorable – and way more fun than a plain old house cat or even a silly pug.

When they'd all stopped laughing, Molly said, "You're a real performer, Niblet. I think this circus stuff is going to be fun for you. Anything exciting happen here today?"

Niblet just blinked behind his glasses. Then he turned his head and blinked at Mrs DeVille's house. "We know," Penelope said. "We saw her."

The monster grunted.

"Try not to let her see you, OK, pal?" Pen said, wrapping her arms around their lovable pet. "We need to keep you – and all our other special secrets – nice and safe."

CHAPTER 6

Booby Traps

"Kids, I have some news." Bree Quirk slid into the back corner booth at Crazy Ed's and emptied her apron's front pocket on to the table. A crumpled pile of dollar bills, about three hundred coins, six order slips and a foil-wrapped chocolate skittered across the table.

Bree had just finished her waitressing shift and was now joining her family for their weekly meal out. Martha Chalupsky – the owner of Crazy Ed's – offered her staff a meal "on Auntie Martha" every week. Free food at a restaurant was always yummy. Especially free food made by Martha, who was an excellent cook.

Bree beamed and began to count her dollar bills. "I'm going on holiday!"

Finn, who'd been hiding under the table, popped up and blurted out, "Huh?"

"Where are we going?" Molly asked, excited. "Somewhere warm?"

"Do we have to take the van?" Penelope added. "Or can we take an aeroplane?"

Bree shook her head and pursed out her lips. "Not *us*, I'm afraid. Just *me*."

"Like, alone?" Molly asked. Her mother had never left them, not for even one night, in all the years they'd been alive. "You're going on a trip without us?"

"I am." Bree smiled proudly. "A few of the other waitresses invited me on a girls' weekend to a lake up north the weekend after next. They play cards and relax and sit in a sauna and do a whole lot of nothing. Doesn't that sound nice?"

Molly agreed that it did sound nice. And sort of

boring. But it also sounded unfair. "Yeah," she said. "I want to go."

"Well, it wouldn't be the same if kids came along," Bree said gently. "I obviously love my little munchkins to bits, but every mum needs a holiday from time to time. Things are going well here in Normal, and I just figured . . ." She looked Penelope in the eye and nodded. "Don't you agree that this will be good for me, dear?"

"I do," Penelope said, smiling. "I'm glad you're making some friends, Mum."

Well, when Penelope put it that way, Molly felt like a real grump for wishing her mum wouldn't go away without them. But she had some serious concerns, too. "Who's going to stay with us?" she asked.

Grandpa Quill grunted. "This guy," he said, thumping his fist on his chest. "I can be in charge." He beat at his chest like a gorilla.

Molly was not reassured. "Gramps is not exactly a responsible adult. No offence, Gramps." She shrugged, and her grandpa shrugged back. "You know how he likes to play with his magic. What if he decides to keep rewinding time, and then the weekend will never be over, and we'll never see you again?"

Bree sighed. "Now, Molly, he couldn't possibly rewind time so much that the end of the weekend will never come. And your grandfather is perfectly capable of keeping a handle on his Quirk to take care of you kids for a few nights."

"Really?" Molly muttered, quietly enough that she thought no one could hear. Everyone knew Grandpa Quill was more like a big kid than a grown adult.

"Really," Bree said. "It's just for a weekend. I never leave you kids, and I think this will be good for me. And for you." She blinked at Molly, waiting for her to argue some more. Molly looked down at the table and began sorting coins instead. "Now, who wants to tell me about school today?"

Molly perked up at this. Then the Quirk kids all talked over one another, each cutting off the others to try to be the first to tell their mum about the Circus of the Dazzling Stars. When it was obvious that they were making no sense at all, Molly and Penelope let Finn tell the story.

Finn spat out everything he had to say in one long breath. "So there's a circus in the gym, and we're going to learn tricks, and I'm going to get to swing on a trapeze in front of the whole town, and I might even get to juggle fire!"

"Well, isn't that nice?" Bree said. "Now, girls, can you please share some additional details?"

Finn crossed his arms over his chest. He didn't like losing his place on centre stage. Molly smiled at him, then shared the whole circus scoop with her mother. Mr Intihar had told the fourth graders that they would be learning trapeze, and juggling, and walking on tightropes and stilts, and riding unicycles, and they might even get to try rolling around inside these crazy wire-ball things.

Then Molly told her mother and Grandpa Quill about the big prize for the best classroom. "The circus people are going to decide which class is the best, and then all those students will get to perform the tricks they've learned in front of the whole school, and all the parents, and the whole town!"

Grandpa Quill looked impressed. "That does sound pretty nifty!" He stroked his moustache.

"The circus is a career I haven't considered. Think I'm too old?"

Penelope laughed. "You're never too old. But I think you like naps too much, Gramps." She covered her mouth. "Oops."

Grandpa chuckled along with her. "That may well be true, kid."

"Don't call me kid," Penelope warned.

"What should I call you? Pipsqueak? Curly?"

"Penelope or dear, sweet, favourite grand-daughter will be fine," Pen said, just as their food arrived.

After they ate, Bree and Grandpa Quirk headed over to the dessert case to take a peek at their options. Martha always had a rotating selection of pies, cakes, cookies and other surprise desserts on display. Finn had figured out that when he was invisible, he could help himself to pretty much anything he wanted in the dessert case – as long as he was sneaky about it. Because he had already eaten part of a piece of pie and several brownie bites that night, he didn't much care what they would choose to share.

As soon as their mother was out of earshot, Finn whispered, "*Psst.*"

"Yes, Finn?" Molly asked, lifting one eyebrow. Penelope looked around uncertainly. When he was invisible, it was always hard for her to figure out where Finn was sitting. At that moment, he was perched in the centre of their table. He had his hands wrapped around a soft wad of mashed potatoes, and he was sculpting it like it was Play-Doh.

"We've got a problem," Finn whispered. He scooted in closer to his sisters and said, "Mrs DeVille."

Molly and Penelope exchanged a look. After what they'd seen her doing that afternoon, Molly and Pen had decided that if they just ignored Mrs DeVille, maybe she would slowly lose interest and stop watching them all the time. "What kind of problem?" Molly asked.

"A big problem," Finn said, holding his arms open wide. The lump of mashed potatoes dropped from his hands and splatted on to the table. "She's a snoop."

"We know," Penelope said, eyeing up the ball of mashed potatoes. "We've seen her peeking."

"Me, too," Finn said with a certain shake of his head. "And I don't like it. Her big, ugly eyeball is always watching me when I'm playing in the garden. Today when Gran and I were hanging the trapeze, she kept peeking at me from her upstairs window. I don't think she saw Gran, though. And it was even worse when I was trying to teach myself how to juggle. Every time one of my beanbags dropped by the fence, it seemed like Mrs DeVille was spying on me through that hole."

After the assembly that day, Finn had come up with the clever idea of setting up a mini circus ring in the Quirks' garden. As soon as he got off the bus, he had begged Grandpa Quill and Gran to help him start setting it up so that he could practise the tricks they would be learning at school when he was at home.

Gran had already helped him hang a trapeze bar from a high-up tree branch, and Grandpa Quill had collected all sorts of things for Finn to try to juggle (so far, he could only manage two beanbags). Next, they were going to stretch a low tightrope between one of the deck rails and the metal clothesline post at the back of the garden. Gran had even offered to sew some costumes so they'd feel like real performers!

Finn scooted off the table and into the booth. He continued speaking quietly. "What if Mrs DeVille does see something – like Niblet? Or Gran? Remember how she said she was going to call the police because she thinks we have a secret? I don't like jail."

"You're not going to jail," Molly reassured him. It wasn't jail she was worried about. It was the possibility that they'd have to move again – flee from the Normal life and friends they'd come to love – that scared Molly more than anything. "We just have to be extra-careful to keep our secrets secret."

Molly glanced over at her mum, who was busy chatting with one of the other waitresses at the coffee counter. Gramps was dancing along to the music from the jukebox, humming to himself. He had a pair of spoons that he kept rapping on the counter to tap out a beat.

"Careful's not gonna cut it," Finn said, sounding like a TV show detective. "We need to be smart." He tapped his potato-crusted fingers on his head, smearing buttery mash in his hair. His mop of sticky-outie hair was even crazier than usual. "We need to come up with a way to keep her out of our B-I-Z business. Set some tricky traps, stuff like that."

"What kind of traps?" Penelope asked, her eyes widening. On the booth beside her, a giant mouse-trap suddenly materialised out of nowhere.

"You mean like booby traps?" Molly suggested. She knew Finn wasn't talking about *actually* trapping their neighbour. She assumed he was talking about making it harder for her to snoop.

Finn giggled. "What's a booby trap?"

"It's a kind of trap you set up to trick someone – or scare them away. Like, if you put a glass of water on top of a door and tied a string to it. Then, when the person opened it, the water would rain down on them. Or if you laid out some bait – maybe a piece of yummy cake – and then when someone grabbed it, a net would fall on their head."

"Ooh," Finn said, his eyes growing wide. "That sounds fun."

Penelope blinked at Molly. "Um, Mol?"

Molly suddenly realised she should *not* have told their brother about booby traps. Finn loved making mischief, and now she'd put a few new ideas into his head. "Forget it," she said. "Booby traps are dangerous."

"Or funny," Finn said, smirking.

"Booby traps aren't going to help us with Mrs DeVille, anyway," Molly said. "She's staying on

her side of the fence, so she's not doing anything wrong. It's not like we can set up traps in
her garden."

"I just wish we could figure out what it is she
thinks she's seen," Penelope mused. "And what she
really is planning to do about it."

"It doesn't *matter* what she's seen," Molly
argued. "As long as Mum's around, we'll be fine.
She can always change Mrs DeVille's mind and
make her forget whatever we need her to forget."

Finn and Penelope both gaped at Molly. Molly
put her hand over her mouth when she realised
why they both looked so terrified. Their mum was
going away in a couple of weeks . . . and without
her Quirk around, they might be in for some serious trouble with nosy Mrs DeVille.

CHAPTER 7

Hep to It

"Ready?"

"Ready!" Penelope hollered. Really, it was more of a squeak than a holler. But that was all she could get to come out of her mouth, considering the situation. The straps of her harness were cinched tight, and her hands were squeezed around a trapeze bar. Her fingers were sweating. She didn't even know fingers *could* sweat, but apparently they could. A lot.

"Hep!" The lead circus instructor, Vivica, tapped Pen's shoulders and gave her a tiny push.

But Penelope paused before she leaped. She wasn't ready to *hep* yet. She looked down. Stella and a couple of other kids from the fourth-grade class were practising walking around on short stilts in the empty area that surrounded the trapeze safety net. Norah was attempting to juggle on the other side of the gym. Nolan, Joey, Raade and some of the other kids in class were trying to climb silk ropes hanging down from tall beams in the corner (mostly, the boys were just swinging wildly to knock one another down). Molly and Izzy kept toppling off the slack rope and tightrope that ran along one wall, about a foot off the floor. Izzy cracked up every time either one of them fell.

Penelope took a breath and glanced down at the trapeze net. Her fingers were so sweaty they felt slimy on the trapeze bar. Even though only a few people were watching Pen, it suddenly felt as if all eyes were on her. When she glanced down again to see if she was right, she saw Molly giving her a thumbs-up.

Penelope hummed and closed her eyes, trying to focus on something other than her own fear and embarrassment. She had to stop freaking herself out, or this whole trapeze thing was going to be a disaster.

"Hep!" Vivica yelled again. Then she whispered, "That means you can go ahead and jump, Miss Quirk. Just a tiny step and you're off."

Pen took one more deep breath, then hopped off the platform. She swung through the air, holding fast to the bar. She wanted so badly to do well.

Poof! Penelope's sweaty fingers and palms went dry again. Rather than feeling as if she might fall, it suddenly felt like her hands were glued to the bar. She tried to lift a finger, and realised that she maybe – probably – *was* glued to the bar. At least she didn't have to worry about plopping down into the net immediately, like most of her class had done during their first try on the trapeze.

Penelope had a sudden vision of herself as a circus star, her body gliding effortlessly through the air. A moment later, Penelope felt herself swinging higher and higher. She heard her classmates gasp as she soared over the net, then back again. She felt free and fantastic, flying through the air. It was almost as though her body had been waiting Pen's whole life to do trapeze.

Swing!

Swing!

In the next instant, Pen's body seemed to take on a life of its own! Her knees pulled up towards her chest. Her legs twisted and bent until they were dangling over the top of the trapeze bar. Suddenly, Penelope's finger glue melted away, and her hands slipped off the bar. She was hanging upside down from a flying trapeze!

"Miss Quirk!" Vivica screamed. "Grab that bar with your hands! We are not doing the knee hangs yet!"

Penelope closed her eyes and tried to take back control of her mind. Her long, curly ponytail dangled down so far that it almost seemed as if it might

graze the safety net. Her hands waved forward and back, which made her swing faster and faster. She had lost all control of her own body – her mind had taken over and turned her into a trapeze superstar.

"Penelope!" Molly cried from over by the slack line. "Focus!"

"Stop letting your imagination take over," Pen whispered to herself. She clenched her teeth and willed her body to cooperate. "Focus." Penelope grabbed the bar with her hands again. She unhooked her legs and let them dangle down. Everyone watching went silent, and in that moment, Pen let go of the bar and dropped down to the net. She landed perfectly.

One little bounce, and she scooted to the edge of the net. She unhooked her safety harness and eased herself to the floor. When she looked up, the whole class was staring at her. In the next moment, everyone started to clap. "I think we have a natural!" Vivica called from up on the platform.

Pen blushed. She hated it when people's attention was focused on her. She preferred to hide behind Molly – who was just a hair taller – and hope no one would notice her at all.

"If the fourth grade wins the chance to perform with us, I think we know who will be flying during your show!" Vivica climbed down the ladder and came over to clap Penelope on the back. "That was a surprise – I take it you've done trapeze before?"

Without thinking, Penelope nodded. *Lie!* Her mind scolded her for fibbing.

"You have? Well, why didn't you say something sooner?" Vivica and the whole fourth-grade class stared at her expectantly.

Pen shrugged. "I don't know. I should have." *Another lie!* She felt her nose beginning to grow longer, like Pinocchio's, with each fib. She knew she had to get out of the spotlight!

"Fourth graders!" Mr Intihar came gliding into the gym like her knight in shining armour. "I know you're all having a great time learning from our circus friends, but I'm afraid it's time to return to the classroom." He clapped his hands three times, a sign that they all needed to line up and stand quietly by the door.

Penelope was first in line. She wanted to get away from the gym as quickly as possible. She hated that the circus stuff was making people pay such close attention to her. She'd loved flying through the air, sure, but she didn't like that she'd made such a spectacle of herself. If Grandpa Quill had been there, she would have begged him to rewind time. She would give anything to go back to the beginning of gym class so she could somehow avoid the trapeze lesson altogether.

But Grandpa wasn't there, and her magic had helped her look like some kind of expert. Now she'd have to swing like a trapeze superstar again the next time. Good thing Finn had set up the rope-and-stick trapeze at home – at least she could practise in the privacy of their garden a little bit. She brightened at the thought that maybe she actually could learn to shine on the trapeze. *Without* her magic to help her.

"Nice moves," Nolan said, stepping into line beside Penelope. "Show-off."

Penelope turned away and tried to ignore him.

"Hey, Circus Quirkus . . . I'm talking to you." Nolan chuckled. He didn't seem to care that Penelope was pointedly trying to ignore him.

"Cut it out," Joey Pahula said, nudging Nolan.

But Nolan kept going. "It's a quirky circ-y! The Quirk Circ!"

Penelope flushed bright red. She was embarrassed, and still shaken from her turn on the flying trapeze. Nolan's teasing was making everything a lot worse. Her mind whirled with thoughts of what she'd like to say and do to make Nolan just *be quiet already*. Her eyes squeezed closed, trying to keep her imagination from racing out of control.

"That will be enough, Mr Paulson." Mr Intihar bent down and looked Nolan right in the eye. After a quick, curt nod of his head, he led the class out of the gym.

Molly caught up with Penelope as the fourth graders followed him down the long, curved hall towards room six. "How cute would Niblet be if he were flying on a trapeze?" This thought made Penelope giggle – and that momentary distraction was enough to get her mind off Nolan for the rest of the afternoon.

CHAPTER 8

Lollipop Spy

Molly and Penelope were in their bedroom working on maths homework after school when the sound of a kazoo drew both girls' eyes to the door. Penelope couldn't see anyone there, but Molly watched as her brother marched past the door of the girls' room, kicking his legs into the air. "I am a Munchkin in Lollipop Land!" Finn sang out, dancing around in the hallway. "I'd like to welcome you to *The Wizard of Oz!*" Molly giggled when she saw his outfit.

"What's he doing?" Pen asked eagerly. As he often was when inside the house, Finn was gumless and invisible. Today, he was also in costume. "Is he all dressed up?"

Finn bowed. Molly eyed him up and down and said, "Well, picture a five-year-old wearing Gramp's trousers. He's also wearing some kind of tartan sweater and a pair of pretzel braces." Molly studied her brother's home-made costume, which was a strange re-creation of a Munchkin outfit from *The Wizard of Oz*.

He had stolen a pair of Grandpa Quill's huge trousers and rolled them up so they were calf length on his scrawny body. Finn had wrapped a long piece of rope around the waist of the slacks to keep them from falling down. It appeared that he'd crafted a pair of braces out of a lot of fat pretzel sticks and some yarn. Molly recognised most of his outfit – except one thing. "Finn, where did you get those socks? Those aren't Mum's."

Finn glanced down at the knee-high socks he was wearing. They were an ugly pink tartan pattern

that looked strangely familiar to Molly. "From Mrs DeVille's drawer," Finn said simply.

Pen gasped. "Finnegan Quirk! Were you *in* Mrs DeVille's house?" She put her hands on her hips and stared angrily at the door. Molly didn't bother to tell her sister that their brother was now lounging on Penelope's bed, picking bits of something out from under his fingernails.

"Sure," Finn answered lazily. "A bunch of times."

"You've been in our neighbour's house *a bunch* of times?" Molly asked. "She's allergic to kids. She really doesn't like us."

"She has cable TV," Finn explained with a shrug. "I like the television shows she watches. They're way better than the stuff Gramps watches after school." He lay back and relaxed his head on Penelope's pillow. "There's this show she watches about circus performers. I'm learning lots from it. Also, she likes game shows. The kind where people cheer and sometimes win fake dogs for a prize. *We* need a fake dog."

Niblet grumbled and rolled out from under Penelope's bed. He plopped his head into

Penelope's lap to remind her that *he* was their pet. "Don't worry, Nibbly," Pen cooed quietly. "You're the only monster for me."

"Does she know you're there?" Molly said, still stunned by Finn's revelation that he'd been hanging out in Mrs DeVille's house. "Do you *talk* to her?"

"She talks to me," Finn said. "At least, she talks to someone. I dunno if she knows I'm there. I'm always quiet. But the thing is, she goes on and on about juggling and walking on a tightrope and cool circus stuff. One day she took a couple of apples out of a bowl on her counter and started juggling them. It was awesome."

"She juggles?" Penelope asked. "Mrs DeVille?"

Finn grinned. "Sure. She's really good at it, too – she doesn't have to use beanbags, even!" He paused. "The thing is, it sort of feels like she's talking to me when I'm there. But I don't talk back." He made an X across his chest and added, "Pinkie promise."

Molly and Penelope both groaned. Their brother definitely should not be poking into other people's houses. *Especially* not Mrs DeVille's house. She was already suspicious of them, and this – well, this could be a disaster. Although Finn was sneaky, he wasn't always quiet, and he was never perfect. What if Mrs DeVille somehow found out someone had been in her house? She'd definitely call the police!

Finn rolled around on Pen's bed and waved his feet in the air. He looked like a kitten playing with a stuffed mouse toy. He carefully peeled the sock off his left foot and began to pluck sticky things out from between his toes. Even Molly didn't notice that he was carefully placing each sticky bit under Penelope's pillow for her to find later. Finn carefully moved the sock to his ear, so it would stay invisible – like the rest of his clothes always were.

"I spotted these socks in her laundry basket the other day. I swiped 'em. She has so many socks that she'll never even notice they're gone. She also has a whole closet full of these awesome costumes, too. Like, hundreds of 'em." Finn held up his right leg and swooped it around in the air, admiring the socks. "These are pretty, huh?"

"I can't see them, so I can't say," Penelope said haughtily. She studied the floor, trying to figure out the exact location of their brother. "But I will say that you should not be in someone's house when you haven't been invited."

Finn rolled his eyes. "She can't see me, so what does it matter?"

"It matters because it's trespassing," Molly agreed. "Finn, you really can't borrow our neighbour's TV. Or her socks."

He pulled the other sock back on. "I'm just using them for one day. It's not like I'm taking them for ever."

"Finn," Molly scolded. "You can't give the socks back after you've worn them."

"So what am I supposed to do? *Steal* them?" Finn

looked horrified. He rolled off Pen's bed and on to the floor, where he curled up right beside Molly.

"For starters, you have to stop going in her house." Molly couldn't believe she actually had to tell her brother that this was a rule. Shouldn't he just *know* that?

"*Pffffffft.*" Finn blew a huge raspberry at his sisters. "I figure it's only fair. If she's going to snoop around our house, I should get to snoop around her house. And since you're both being so bossy about it, I guess I won't tell you what I heard today when I was there."

Molly perked up at this. "What did you hear?"

"Will you tell everyone that I'm a super-spy?"

"Spill, Finn."

Finn sighed deeply. "Fine. I heard her on the phone today."

"Mrs DeVille?"

"Of course Mrs DeVille! How many houses do you think I'm sneaking into?"

Molly shrugged. "So what did you hear?"

"I heard her . . ." He leaned in close to Molly, then took a bite out of one of his pretzel braces.

". . . on the phone. She was talking to someone from the TV!"

Pen gasped. "About what?"

"She told them they should get some cameras over here and check stuff out. Get some leggage. That's what she said, exactly."

"Leggage?" Penelope wondered aloud.

"Do you mean 'footage'?" Molly asked. "Footage is what reporters call the videos they show on the news."

"Oh, yeah," Finn said. "It was footage. She told them to come and get *foot*age of her neighbours."

Molly sighed. "Is that everything?"

"Nope," Finn said. "But first say I'm the bestest spy in Normal."

"Fine," Molly agreed. "You're an excellent spy. What else did you hear?"

"She also told someone on the phone that her neighbour has a weird pet." Finn looked puzzled. "I guess Mrs DeVille's neighbour on the other side must have a cool animal. Maybe I should sneak into that family's house and check it out. I hope it's a lizard." He chewed at his lip, obviously planning his next adventure. Then he looked up and said, "At least we're not the only neighbours she's spying on."

"I bet she *is* talking about us," Molly said, frowning. "I'm sure she's talking about Niblet!" Her eyes grew wide, and she sucked in a breath. "What if she called Animal Control or something? What if she's trying to get them to come and take him away?"

Finn shrugged. "Dunno." He bent forward to take another bite out of his pretzel braces.

Penelope scooted across the floor and reached her arm under her bed. Niblet dropped a limp paw in her hand. "No one can take Niblet," she whispered. "She couldn't make someone take Niblet from us. Could she?"

"No way," Molly said. But she wasn't so sure. Because no one could know for certain just how much mean old Mrs DeVille had seen – or what she really might do.

CHAPTER 9

Glue Trick Kick

"Finn!" Molly screamed from the bathroom a few days later. "Not *again*!" She tugged at the toilet seat lid, but it refused to open. Ever since his afternoon of snooping at Mrs DeVille's house, Finn had been obsessed with setting booby traps to keep people out of their house.

But Finn's pranks did nothing more than torture the whole Quirk family. For the past few days, he had been on a glue trick kick – super-glue, hot-glue gun, plain white school glue, it really didn't matter. Finn enjoyed playing with *any* glue.

His first prank had actually been pretty clever, even Molly had to admit. Invisible, Finn had sneaked around the breakfast table and glued down Grandpa's coffee cup between sips. Grandpa reached over to grab it and discovered his mug was stuck to the table – permanently. He tried to rewind time to get it *un*stuck, but Finn kept doing the same thing over and over and over again until Grandpa just gave up. (Three days later, the mug was still there . . . and the coffee inside was starting to get a little mouldy.)

The next day, he'd glued one of Molly's flip-flops to the floor. When she slipped it on and tried to take a step, she fell flat on her face.

Just yesterday, he'd discovered how much fun could be had in the bathroom. First, he'd slathered white school glue all over the edges of the toilet paper. But he'd used too much, and instead of gluing the paper to the roll, he'd just created a goopy, squelchy mess on the bathroom floor. Before bed, he'd used the hot-glue gun to fuse the toilet seat closed. Gramps had to use a flathead screwdriver to pry the lid open, leaving a scratchy ring of dried-up glue bits all over the seat.

Today, apparently, he'd done it again. Molly stormed out of the bathroom into the upstairs hall and stomped to the door of Finn's room. "Finnegan Quirk! You've got to stop gluing the toilet lid down! It's disgusting."

Finn smirked. "It's funny. Booby traps are awesome."

Molly growled at him. But it was hard for her to stay mad, since she was the one who had told him about booby traps in the first place. He was just having some fun. At least his pranks were contained in the house – it wasn't like he was setting rope traps outside for Mrs DeVille and her sneaky news reporters and monster-stealing friends.

"Mr Intihar and Charlie are coming over in ten minutes," Molly hissed. "You'd better fix the toilet before they get here. Mum's already nervous enough about having friends over for dinner – if we don't have a working bathroom, she's going to freak."

"They can piddle in the garden," Finn argued. "No biggie."

Molly groaned. "They cannot *piddle* in the garden. And neither can I. Fix it, Finn, and stop booby-trapping your own family."

Finn laughed. "Gramps will help me fix it," he said. "He loves my tricks."

"I'm sure he does," Molly muttered. Grandpa Quill was a big fan of pranks. In fact, Molly had overheard Grandpa Quill and Finn giggling about other booby traps they were planning. They really cracked each other up.

"We need to prepare, Molly." Finn chomped on

his gum and leaned down to pull at a piece of fraying carpet in the hall. "What if a reporter tries to sneak into our house to spy on us? We have to keep him *out*."

"A reporter isn't going to sneak into our house." Molly sighed. "A reporter would knock on the door." Even as she said it, she wondered if that was true. It sounded true.

"What if someone comes to take Niblet?" Finn asked, his eyes huge. "You're the one who told me someone might come and get him. What if it's someone mean? A big, bad guy could sneak in and steal him from us – someone like that Animal Control guy you were talking about."

Molly sighed again. Penelope had been worrying about the same thing for the past few days. Her sister had even started letting Niblet sleep under the covers at the foot of her bed at night, just to make sure he was safe while they slept. "No one is going to sneak into our house, Finn. You just don't need to worry about that." But deep down, she was a little nervous, too. Also, she felt bad for Finn, since she remembered being five.

That was the year their dad left – he'd tucked

the girls into their beds one night, but when they woke the next morning, he was gone. Without their dad around, Molly and Penelope spent a lot of time worrying about monsters and mean guys and sneaks in the house, too. And they still worried a lot – about Penelope's magic, fitting in at school, and when they would have to move next.

"How do you *know*, Molly?" Finn looked at Molly hopefully, waiting for some certain answer, a promise that he could stop fretting about sneaks and thieves and snoops and other things that might go bump in the night. But Molly couldn't promise anything.

"I just do," she said. "Now go and unstick the toilet and hand over the glue gun, big guy."

Finn returned to his room and dug a box of various glue containers out from under his bed. "Can I keep a few bottles?" He flashed her a mostly toothless smile. Little nubs of new front teeth had begun to grow in, and the stubby little teeth made Finn look awfully cute and charming. "For craft projects?"

Molly shook her head, not fooled by his goofy smile. "No more glue."

"Fine." Finn stuck out his tongue. "But Gramps and I can booby-trap without glue. Just you wait and see!" He skipped to the bathroom and pounded at the glued-down toilet lid like it was a snare drum.

Molly hustled downstairs to help her mum and Penelope finish cooking dinner. The Quirks were having their very first ever dinner party at their house. Bree and the girls' teacher – Mr Call-Me-George Intihar – had become friends. It just so happened that Mr Intihar had a son, Charlie, who was Finn's age. Charlie usually lived with his mum in another nearby town, but he and Finn had got to be friends the last time Charlie had come to stay with his dad.

"Molly, can you please set the table?" Bree was rushing around the kitchen, doing several dozen things at once. It was an absolute disaster zone, with dishes piled on top of dishes and clumps of flour stuck to the floor. There were two pots of boiling water, a pan of red sauce was bubbling away, and there were at least two cakes and a pie baking in the oven. Penelope was whipping up a batch of cream-cheese icing for the carrot-cake muffins they'd baked earlier in the day.

"Sure, Mum. What else can I help with?"

"Get out a jug for water, and . . . *Oh!* Can you make some lemonade? Also, could you just run outside and see if your gran has any of those nice edible flowers left in the garden? I know she planted a few when we moved in to see if they'd survive the end of the season. I thought it might be nice to add some pretty colour to the salad." Bree stopped spinning around the kitchen for a moment and stood perfectly still. It was as though she'd been sucked into the eye of a tornado and was experiencing a moment of calm before the whole kitchen exploded again.

Molly looked at her mother closely and realised – not for the first time – just how beautiful Bree was. Her hair was curly, like Molly's and Pen's. It was often sticking up here and there in a wild and frizzy kind of way, but that just added to her charm. She had a face that made people want to smile. And the way she looked at a person – like they were the only person on earth – made you feel like luck was on your side, just because you were around her. Bree often said her natural charm was simply a side effect of her Quirk. When people spent a lot of time with her, it seemed as though they were under a spell. But Molly knew her mum was amazing, Quirk or not.

"Mum, it's going to be a great dinner," Penelope said, trying to shake her mother out of her cooking trance.

Molly dipped a finger into her sister's mixing bowl and licked a bit of frosting. "Yeah, it will be fun having friends over for dinner."

"You're right, girls," Bree said, smiling. "It's just strange, you know? We've never had guests at our house. I want it all to go perfectly."

"It will," Molly said, tucking a flyaway curl behind her sister's ear. Then Bree swept over and wrapped both of her girls into a hug.

With her face squished between her mother and sister, Molly added, "I'm sure everything will be fine." As she headed for the back door to see if her gran had anything pretty that they could use in their salad, Molly gave her mum a reassuring smile.

She reached out and opened the door to the garden. But when she went to step outside, she bounced backwards instead. *Wham!* The whole door frame had been covered in clear plastic wrap. She could still see through the door to the outside, but there was no way through. "Finn . . ." Molly muttered as she pulled at the tape that held cling film to the door frame.

Her brother's booby traps were starting to be a real problem.

A Tornado in the Kitchen

CHAPTER 10 ←

Just as Molly peeled the last bits of plastic wrap off the back door, the front doorbell rang. She hustled into the hall. Mr Intihar stood on the porch, smiling behind a big bouquet of autumn flowers.

"Hello, Miss Molly," he said. After a pause, he added, "Say hello, Charlie." Mr Intihar nudged his son into the Quirks' front hall. Charlie had a large polka-dotted golf visor pulled low over his forehead. He was also wearing a pair of black plastic 3-D glasses, for no apparent reason.

Charlie stared at Molly as though he didn't quite remember her from Normal Night. Finally, he waved at her and said, "Howdy, dude."

"Come on in," Molly said. "Dinner's almost ready. Do you, um, want to hang out in the living room for a few minutes until it's time to eat?" Molly glanced into the living room, wishing she'd let her mother open the door. She wasn't sure what to do with their guests now that they'd arrived.

Grandpa Quill, who had been helping Finn with the gluey toilet seat, was now slumbering on the couch in front of the TV. Several pairs of dirty socks were strewn about the room, along with a collection of blankets and an open board game and some half-finished puzzles. The armchair was piled high with clean laundry that sat waiting to be folded. There was absolutely nowhere to sit, unless Mr Intihar wanted to lift up Grandpa's feet and slip in under them.

"Don't be silly," Mr Intihar said. "I'm not going to sit around and kick my feet up while your mum's cooking. I'd be happy to help."

Molly grimaced. The living room was bad, but she knew the kitchen was worse. She led her teacher and Charlie towards the disaster area. Penelope cut them off at the kitchen door, trapping their guests in the dining room. She quickly said hello, then pulled Molly aside to whisper, "I just made a whole pot of sauce explode all over the kitchen."

Molly laughed and whispered back, "It sort of looks like a tornado hit in there. Mum's not exactly a clean-as-you-go sort of cook."

"I thought it looked like a tornado hit, too!" Pen whispered. "And then, *whoops* . . . that's sort of what happened."

Molly shrugged. "There's not much we can do about it now. At least they weren't here when it happened." She smiled at Mr Intihar, who was giving them a curious look. "It's a bit of a mess in the kitchen," Molly explained as she and Penelope stepped aside to let their guests pass through into the cooking zone.

"Well, hello!" Bree chirped. She seemed almost oblivious to the disaster in the kitchen. "Don't mind this wee bit of mess." She focused on Mr Intihar's eyes, then turned her attention to Charlie. "A mess in the kitchen means it will be a tastier meal." She winked.

Molly wasn't sure if her mum was using her magic or not, but neither of their guests seemed to notice that they were surrounded by sticky floors and heaps of dirty dishes and the dripping red remains of what was supposed to be their pasta sauce.

"We'll be ready to eat in just a few minutes.

George, would you be so kind as to help the girls set the table? Charlie, why don't you head on upstairs and find Finn? He's been waiting for you to arrive."

"OK, dude," Charlie said. He rubbed his fingers over his 3-D glasses, then dashed off. Molly heard the third stair squeak violently as Charlie leaped from the bottom of the staircase up to the third step.

Penelope grabbed plates and cups, wiping each item off as she handed it to her teacher. When you were eating on dishes at the Quirk house, you could never be too careful. Finn sometimes helped wash up, and when he did, bits of dinner often stayed on the plate until the next time they came out of the cupboard.

"How are you enjoying the circus lessons?" Mr Intihar asked as he worked with Molly and Penelope.

"They're super-fun," Molly answered. She was going to ask him if the circus people had said anything about which grade was doing best, but suddenly a huge *thud* boomed above them. Bree popped her head into the dining room and looked around curiously. Then she and Mr Intihar dashed through the dining room towards the stairs.

"Finn?" Bree called, skidding into the front hall.

"Charlie?" Mr Intihar yelled from behind her. "Everything OK up there?"

"We're OK!" Finn said, his voice echoing. Molly hoped everything *else* was fine up there, too – like Niblet. Their lovable furry pet often found himself in sticky situations with Finn. And Charlie was *not* supposed to know about Niblet.

"Where *are* you?" Molly heard Charlie's muffled voice say. "Finn? I can't see you, dude. Are you hiding? What's going on?"

Molly gulped. Her brother had obviously decided to take out his gum. She knew he had probably gone invisible. He loved trying to trick people who didn't know about his Quirk. And Charlie seemed like the kind of kid who'd be easily tricked.

A moment later, as the adults rushed for the stairs to check on the two boys, Molly heard someone stumble. Mr Intihar muttered "*Oof!*" just as something screeched overhead. The screech was followed by a loud splatting sound. Molly and Penelope both yelped. Then they dashed out of the dining room and into the front hall to see what had happened.

Mr Intihar stood stock-still on the first step with a face full of whipped cream and pumpkin pie. He swiped a finger across each eye so he could see through the sweet, sticky mess.

Grandpa Quill peered around the corner from the living room. There was a barely concealed grin on his face. "Looks like that booby trap worked," he mused.

"Really, Dad?" Bree said, obviously annoyed. "Are you responsible for this?"

"Not me!" Grandpa insisted, holding his hands up in the air. "Talk to young Finnegan. I'm just the lowly assistant. He's the brains behind this booby-trap business."

Bree rolled her eyes and started to march up the stairs again. "He's five," she snapped. "You're *sixty*-five."

Finn thundered down the stairs as Bree stomped up. When Finn saw Mr Intihar with a messy

white and orange face, he cheered. "That booby trap worked!" Then he saw the look on his mother's face. He slouched down and muttered, "Gramps can rewind us back a little bit and fix it, easy peasy."

Before anyone could say anything more, Molly felt time whoosh backwards. A moment later she was back in the dining room with Penelope and Mr Intihar. The *thud* came from above them again. Molly followed as Bree and Mr Intihar jogged into the front hall. This time, Grandpa was peeking around the corner, watching them gleefully from the living room.

"Finn?" Bree called, again.

"Charlie?" Mr Intihar repeated. "Everything OK up there?"

"We're OK!" Finn hollered.

"They're fine – " Molly started to say. Just as she was about to warn her mum and teacher *not* to climb the stairs, Penelope hustled past all of them. She zoomed into the front hall, hopped on to the first stair, tripped on a rope, and something screeched above her. Moments later, the pumpkin pie swung through the air again, narrowly missing her face. It swung back towards her again and smushed into the back of Pen's hair. Mr Intihar and Bree both rushed over to help her.

"Not again!" Molly growled, narrowing her eyes at Grandpa Quill. She couldn't believe the same booby trap had got both Mr Intihar *and* Penelope.

"I'll rewind one more time," Grandpa told Molly, chuckling. "And this time, I promise to deactivate the trap so no one gets pie faced. I just wanted to watch it happen live once, for funsies. Pie face is hilarious."

Grandpa screwed up his mouth, and a second later, Molly found herself in the dining room again. This time, as soon as the *thud* rang out above them, Molly shouted, "Pen and I will go check on the boys!" Mr Intihar and Bree both looked worried. "Really," Molly said, "I'm positive they're fine. We'll stay up there and make sure they're not getting into any kind of trouble."

"Thank you, dear," Bree said, patting Molly on the shoulder. "That would be lovely. George and I will finish up dinner." She looked distracted as she turned back towards the kitchen. "I need to find some new pasta sauce, since the one that's been simmering all afternoon is on the floor."

Once the adults had gone back to the kitchen, Molly stepped timidly on to the first step, followed by her sister. Then they moved to the second. And the third, and so on. Molly breathed a deep sigh of relief when they made it all the way up without a face full of pumpkin pie.

CHAPTER 11

Oopsie Trapsie!

"Finn?" Molly called as she stepped into the upstairs hall. "Charlie?"

Penelope glanced around, trying to figure out which direction the thud had come from. "Where are you guys?"

"I'm right here!" Finn said, bounding out of the bathroom. "Silly ducks. I was just hiding from Charlie!" He blew a huge bubble with his fresh piece of gum. "That dude can't see anything through those glasses. He doesn't even notice when I go invisible."

"What was the loud noise?" Pen asked, peeking at her bedroom door. It was open just the tiniest bit, and Niblet's round eyeball was staring out at them through the crack. She and Molly had begged their monster to please – pretty please – hide for the night. "If Mr Intihar or Charlie sees you," Penelope had explained, "they might tell people about you. And then something bad could happen."

Niblet had nodded as though he understood. The girls had given him a big bowl of olives and popcorn (his favourite snack) and promised him he could sleep in Pen's bottom bunk while they were having dinner. They'd also promised to help him with his juggling, if only he'd behave. Niblet loved to eat snacks under Penelope's bunk, and he *really* loved learning the kids' circus tricks, but he was also very curious. He wasn't used to the Quirks having dinner guests, and his curiosity had got the best of him.

"Clearly, he doesn't realise how obvious he is, peeking out at us like that," Molly said, pointing.

Niblet was wearing Pen's tutu yet again. Grinning, their monster opened the bedroom door a bit farther and stepped partway into the hall. He had a beanbag balanced on his head, and two more were nestled in his hands. Finn, Molly and Penelope watched as their monster threw the beanbags up into the air. As he tried to juggle the two bags, Niblet's little tongue lolled from the corner of his mouth. Over the past few days, their monster had really got into the action with the kids' circus practise. Usually, the Quirk kids loved seeing his little performances, but it was an absolutely terrible moment for him to come out and perform.

Penelope crept towards the girls' bedroom and nudged her monster's teensy toes back into the bedroom with her own foot. Then she eased the door closed. Niblet whined from inside the bedroom. "Sorry, pal," Pen whispered. "I just want to keep you safe. We don't want anyone to take you." Niblet let out a terrified shriek, followed by several sad sobs – they knew he didn't want anyone to take him, either. He was afraid of everything, except the spooky dark space under Penelope's bed. The girls heard the beanbags land with a *plop plop plop* on the floor in their bedroom, followed by a louder *plop* as Niblet dropped into the beanbag chair in the corner.

Molly turned to Finn. "Where on earth did Charlie go?"

Charlie's voice rang out from behind Finn's bedroom door. "Hey, dudes. I'm in here." Molly poked her head around the corner. Charlie was on the floor, limbs askew, with his body tangled up tight in a Star Wars bedsheet. His visor was crooked and his

3-D glasses had been knocked to the back of his head. "The world is flat," he said, staring at Molly. He shook his head sadly. "No more 3-D."

Finn ploughed into his bedroom and leaped on to his friend. "I did more booby traps! I totally got Charlie with that cake trick you told me about, Molly. I laid a carrot-cake muffin out like bait, and he fell for it. Grabbed it, and the sheet plopped down on him. He was so surprised, he fell over and everything. My trap trick worked!"

Molly had been worried about the Quirk family magic making things difficult for their dinner party. She hadn't even considered the trouble their brother would cause with his silly pranks. "Cool it with the booby traps, Finn," Molly said. "Dinner's almost ready. Mum's going to kill you if you ruin this night for her."

Finn stuck out his tongue. Molly and Pen both helped untangle Charlie from Finn's trap, then the boys reluctantly followed them downstairs. As the girls helped Mr Intihar finish setting the table, Charlie sang to himself and Finn entertained everyone with his new favourite joke. "What kind of nut is always going to the bathroom?" he asked, hopping up and down. When no one answered, Finn cried out, "A peanut!"

Mr Intihar laughed, but Molly was pretty sure he was just being polite. Grandpa also chuckled, then rewound time so that he – and unfortunately,

Molly - could hear the joke again. "What kind of nut is always going to the bathroom?" Finn repeated, the same silly smile plastered to his face. "A peanut!"

After they'd finished dinner and everyone had cake and pie - they all got double dessert, thanks to Grandpa Quill - Mr Intihar patted his stomach. "I'm absolutely stuffed. I think I should have stopped *before* dessert," he said. "It's still so nice out, and I'm not sure we have a lot of these nights left. Maybe a long walk will help me burn off some of that delicious pie."

"I'd love to join you," Bree said, quickly standing up. "Dad, you'll take care of these dishes." It was an order rather than a question. Bree rarely used her magic on her own family. But when the kitchen looked like it did, Molly could understand why her mother would make someone else deal with it. Grandpa Quill quickly made his way to the kitchen and started a sink full of soapy water.

"Mu-*um*," Finn whined. "We've been stuck hanging out with you at this table for the last hour. I sat still and everything. Can't Charlie and I just go upstairs and play with my Lego? Grandpa can keep an eye on us." There was a mischievous glint in his eye that made Molly nervous. Charlie sat beside him, fiddling with his visor and glasses.

"That's fine," Bree said.

But Molly had a feeling it wouldn't be fine. It wasn't until she went to clear the table, and found that every single plate had been glued into place, that she knew her hunch was right. "You know what, Mum? Maybe Pen and I should hang out here and keep an extra eye on Finn and Charlie," Molly said, shrugging off her sweatshirt. Molly looked over at her brother and saw that an actual extra eye had *poof*ed out of nowhere and landed on Finn's back.

"Maybe she's right," Pen blurted, talking over Molly. She squeezed her eyes closed, and the eye that had been on Finn's back melted into thin air.

"OK, girls," Bree said, wrapping a scarf tightly around her neck. Mr Intihar held the door open for her, and they went out into the chilly-but-nice night. "We'll be back in a bit."

As soon as the door closed behind their mum

and Mr Intihar, Molly and Penelope hustled upstairs. First, they checked to see that Niblet was still hidden out of view. They were dismayed to see that he had propped himself up with a pile of cushions and sat curled up in the girls' little window seat. He had finished his snack and was now chewing on a pair of Pen's socks as he prasticed his juggling. The curtains on both windows were flung wide open, letting the inky night squeeze into their brightly lit room. "Niblet! The whole world can see you." Molly hustled over and pulled the curtains closed. "You know we have to be careful. Mrs DeVille could be watching us."

Niblet pulled his fluffy eyebrows together behind his big, smudgy glasses. He looked embarrassed and angry. Sniffling, he slipped under Pen's bed and began to cry. For a monster, Niblet was way too sensitive.

Pen reached under the bed and stroked his fur. Niblet's smooshy body was sort of rough. He was usually fluffy and soft, but Finn had shaved the monster's fur with Grandpa's electric razor a few weeks earlier. Niblet still looked a little silly and

got chilled easily. Pen pushed a blanket under the bed and Niblet curled up inside it. Their monster had always been a comfort to Penelope when she was feeling sad and scared and guilty about her magical mishaps. Now Pen liked having an opportunity to return the favour for her friendly pet.

Molly turned off the overhead light in their room. She pulled back a corner of the curtain and peeked out into the blackness of the evening. Pen pressed her face against Molly's for a look, too. Sure enough, Mrs DeVille was standing in the downstairs window of her house. Their neighbour's body was positioned so she had a perfect view up into Molly and Penelope's room. A pair of binoculars was wrapped around her neck, and a large cordless phone was pressed up against her ear.

"OK," Molly said with a sigh, letting the curtain fall closed again. "We've definitely got a problem."

CHAPTER 12

Sneaky Snoop

"Why can't she just mind her own business?" Penelope groaned. "What we do in *our* house and *our* garden is none of her business."

"But she thinks it is," Molly said.

"It's not polite to stare at people and butt into their business," Pen muttered. "Shouldn't she know that?"

Molly flopped down on her sister's bed. Niblet grumbled as the springs squished down on his furry body. "Maybe she feels like neighbours are allowed to be curious." Molly didn't know why she was making excuses for Mrs DeVille. But Penelope worried an awful lot, and she knew it was probably best to downplay Mrs DeVille's snooping.

"There's a difference between curious and nosy," Pen countered. "That lady's just nosy. Do you think she's really going to get a reporter to come over here? Or Animal Control?" Pen looked scared.

Molly laughed uneasily. "That's crazy –" Just as she was about to tease her sister for worrying too much, thinking the whole idea of someone taking a *monster* was ridiculous, a bright light flashed outside the girls' window.

"Someone's out there!" Penelope said, her eyes growing wide. "Was that a torch? Or the flash from a camera?"

Molly felt her bellyful of pie churn with nerves. "It's probably just Mrs DeVille doing something in her garden." She peered out from behind the curtain again. Mrs DeVille was no longer standing in the window. Her curtains were now closed up tight, and she was nowhere to be seen.

"Or maybe it's Mum," Molly suggested, hoping

she was right. She didn't like the idea that was growing in her mind – the thought that it possibly *could* be some sort of stranger poking around outside their house, trying to get a peek at Niblet and their other secrets. "Finn?" Molly called out to her brother. When there was no answer, she comforted herself with the idea that their brother was probably just playing torch tag in the side garden or something. "I'll go and check it out," Molly said, standing up.

"I'm coming with you," Pen said, trailing behind Molly.

Molly stopped before she reached the door. "Niblet, buddy," she called, walking back into the room to tap her foot under Penelope's bunk. "You awake under there?"

Niblet awoke with a start. He grunted and rolled to the furthest corner beneath the bed.

"Just stay there, OK?" Molly peeked below the bed. "You keep sleeping and stay out of sight, and we'll do our best to keep you safe."

Niblet blinked at her in the darkness. He looked scared.

"There's nothing for you to worry about, big guy. We won't let anyone take you." Niblet whined and burrowed further back into the corner.

"OK," Molly said, mostly to calm herself. Then both girls stepped into the upstairs hall. Behind Finn's closed door, they could hear their brother and Charlie digging through a box of Lego. Charlie kept exclaiming, "Dude!"

Molly turned Finn's doorknob and poked her head around the door frame. "Finn?"

"Yeah?" Finn said.

"Are you guys playing with torches?"

Finn shook his head. "Nuh-uh. Do you have some? Charlie and I could make a fort." Charlie stared at the girls through his dark 3-D glasses. It was a wonder he could see anything at all.

Molly and Penelope shared a look. They hadn't heard their mum coming back. And if Finn hadn't been outside with a torch . . . who was it?

The girls tiptoed back into their bedroom and looked out of their other window, the one that overlooked the garden. Grandpa Quill was

sitting on the deck, his legs tucked under a blanket. Gran was nestled in his hand. Grandpa Quill had one iPod earbud tucked inside his ear, and Gran was holding the other one in her lap like a tiny radio. Grandpa and Gran Quirk liked to spend evenings on the back deck together. They would sit for hours, enjoying the view of Gran's gardens.

Suddenly, Molly heard the front door squeak

open. "Mum?" Molly yelled, stepping out into the hall. "Mr Intihar? Is that you?"

There was no answer. The loose floorboard in the front hall creaked. Pen wrapped her hand around Molly's arm and then grabbed her sister's hand. "I'm scared," she whispered.

Finn peeked out into the hallway. "What's going on?" he blurted out. "Why are you holding hands like that?"

"I think someone's in the house," Molly whispered back. She clutched Penelope's hand tightly in her own, trying to keep her sister's imagination from running wild and making this whole situation worse.

"Gramps is down there," Finn said. "Doing dishes."

"Gramps is out on the back deck with Gran. And we're pretty sure we just heard someone open the front door." Penelope began to shake. In the next instant, all three Quirk kids were wearing battle gear. Metal chest plates, shields and *Star Wars* Stormtrooper helmets popped out of thin air and landed on their bodies.

Charlie stepped out into the hall. "What's with the costumes?" he asked, his little voice cutting through the quiet in the hall. He pushed his visor up on his forehead and adjusted his glasses. "Are we playing dressing-up?"

"Shhh!" Molly, Pen and Finn all shushed him.

"You think someone's *in* our house?" Finn asked, his eyes wide. "Do I need to get all my booby traps ready? Is it time to put my master plan into action?"

A moment later, the third step groaned under someone's – or something's – weight. The kids could only see the top three steps from the upstairs hallway. So if something *was* down there, they wouldn't know what they were up against until it was too close to do anything about it. Pen's eyes got wide as another stair groaned.

"There isn't time, Finn," Molly said. Now she regretted not letting her brother go crazy booby-trapping the whole house. If someone really had managed to sneak in, at least they could have trapped whoever it was until they could get help – and hide Niblet. But instead, they were all stuck upstairs with only some silly battle gear

– and a pair of 3-D glasses – to protect them. "You guys go into Finn's room," Molly said to Charlie and Finn, trying to sound much braver than she felt. "We'll let you know when you can come out."

Finn's eyes were wide and watery. "Is it a bad guy? Is it Animal Control?"

"I don't know," Molly said. There was a scratch on the floorboards, and all four of them screamed.

Charlie shrugged and muttered "Dude" before hustling into Finn's room. He didn't seem all that concerned. In fact, it seemed like his head was in the clouds rather than on the second floor of the Quirks' house. Molly was relieved *she* was the one thinking that, rather than her sister.

Finn pulled off his Stormtrooper mask and tucked his gum behind his ear. The lines of his body shivered out of view. A moment later, he tugged at a rope that Molly hadn't noticed hanging down from the hall ceiling. A net – which looked suspiciously like a piece of the old football goal they'd found in the garage – flopped out from behind the hall table and flew over their heads. It dangled over the stairs, ready to plop down on whoever was trying to sneak up on them.

The girls' bedroom door squeaked open, and Niblet peeked into the hall. He took a tentative step out of the room. Molly shoved him back inside to keep him away from prying eyes.

A shadow slipped around the bend in the stairs, and they all froze. Then Finn wrapped his arms and legs around the rope, tugged, and dropped his net – straight on to the intruder!

CHAPTER 13

Mini Monster

Invisible Finn leaped off the top step and dropped on to the pile of netting that was heaped on the stair landing. Molly couldn't see much under Finn's trap, but she did know that whatever they had trapped was tiny. She couldn't make out legs or arms or even a face under the piles and piles of twisted-up rope.

"Finn, be careful," Molly warned, rushing down to pull her brother off his trap. Sometimes, Finn forgot that invisibility wasn't the same as invincibility. He could still get hurt. Suddenly, the tense fear of the past few minutes crumbled, and Molly found herself feeling like she wanted to cry.

"What did we catch?" Penelope whispered from the top of the steps. "Who is it?"

Both Molly and Finn stepped away from the trap on the landing and pulled at a corner of the netting. Inside the booby trap was a mini monster, one that was about as tall as a footstool. The monster had blunt blue claws, a bright purple stomach and fluffy mud-coloured fur that was speckled with yellow spots, and was wearing a ten-eyed cat-burglar mask. Every one of the monster's ten gleaming eyes was looking at them. Whatever it was, it was downright cute. "What *is* that?" Finn asked, poking at the monster.

The monster poked back, and Finn giggled. He poked again, and the monster poked back again. This went on and on, until they were both rolling around and giggling on the stair landing.

"My fault," Pen said sadly from her perch on the top step. "I guess my imagination just got worked up. After we saw Mrs DeVille peeking at us again tonight, I had this spooky idea that maybe some-one or something would try to sneak up on us. This guy –" she pointed to the monster – "is the monster that was chasing me in a dream one night earlier this week. Sorry, guys."

Charlie poked his head around Finn's bedroom door and asked, "Is it safe to come out yet?"

"Oh!" Molly said, rushing back up the top three stairs. How on earth were they supposed to explain a mini monster trapped inside a net on their stair landing? "Yeah, Charlie, everything's fine." She turned to peek back down the stairs and saw that the mini monster was gone again – disappeared in a *poof*, just the way it had appeared in the first place. "False alarm. We thought we heard footsteps, but it was just my imagination."

"Actually, mine," Pen mumbled.

"Can we play Lego again?" Charlie asked. "Where's Finn?"

Molly looked at her brother, who was still completely invisible on the stair landing. "He'll be right back."

"OK," Charlie said with a shrug. He pushed his dark glasses back up on his face. "I'll keep building." He returned to Finn's room without another word.

Finn gathered up his trap supplies and popped gum into his mouth again. "I told you the booby traps were a good idea," he said proudly. "We caught something, didn't we?"

"We caught a monster that was a figment of Penelope's imagination," Molly argued. "Not a news reporter or Animal Control or Mrs DeVille."

"Still," Finn huffed. "We caught it. If it *had* been a bad guy, I would have been a hero."

"You would have been a hero," Molly agreed with a smile. "Our booby-trapping hero. Thanks, Finn."

She and Penelope returned to their room, while Finn went back to playing Lego with Charlie. "So you're really worried, huh?" Molly asked Penelope, once they were curled up on one end of Pen's bed. Molly tossed another pair of socks to Niblet, who was again hidden in the darkest corner under their bunk beds.

"Yeah," Penelope admitted. "It's creepy, the way she's always watching us."

"Do you think she'll figure out our secrets?" Molly asked.

Pen shrugged. "I'm worried about what she's seen and how much she knows. And you just admitted that we really do have to worry about a news reporter sneaking up on us. It scares me more, knowing you're worried about it, too." Pen pulled her legs in close and wrapped her arms around her body. She turned to rest her cheek on her knee so she could look at her sister. "Everything about our life feels different in Normal than it has in other towns. I don't want to be forced to leave just because Mrs DeVille is poking around."

"Do you think we should tell Mum?" Molly asked.

Penelope shook her head. "About Mrs DeVille? No way. What good would it do?"

"Worst-case scenario," Molly said slowly. "She'll make us move again. Pack up and leave Normal. That's what we always do when someone finds out about us."

"Exactly," Pen said. "And best-case scenario? She'll definitely refuse to go on her weekend away with the other Crazy Ed's waitresses so she can be here if there's any trouble. I don't want to be the reason she cancels her trip. I'd feel so guilty!"

Molly sort of did want their mother to stay home, but she knew she couldn't say it. "So we agree not to tell her?"

Pen nodded.

"We can handle it, right?" Molly asked, hoping for some reassurance. Penelope said nothing. After a moment of silence, Molly said, "I do have one idea. Maybe we could ask Gran about Mrs DeVille. She's outside all the time, and she probably sees more than we even realise."

"That's a great idea. She loves to help." Pen leaped off the bed. "Let's talk to her now."

"Now?" Molly said, yawning. Niblet had poked one of his big, squishy paws up from under the bed, and Molly was stroking it almost like a normal kid would pet an ordinary cat. Niblet made a funny *glub-glub* sound when he was happy and warm, and Molly didn't want to disappoint him by getting up and leaving. "We can talk to her in the morning."

"But it's all I can think about *tonight*," Pen argued. "Do you really want me to keep imagining the worst possible things?"

Molly pushed Niblet's paw off her lap. "Good point." She knew she definitely did *not* want her sister to keep imagining things that went bump in the night. They already had their fair share of monsters in the house.

CHAPTER 14

Super-Size Gran

When the girls got downstairs, they immediately realised that Grandpa Quill had not cleaned the kitchen. But he *had* begun to fill a sink full of soapy water right after dinner. Then he'd obviously got distracted and forgotten to turn off the tap. Because now bubbling fingers of soapy suds stretched into the dining room, and water pooled in the corners of the room where the floors of their old house slanted and dipped.

"Oh!" Molly gasped when the girls hustled into the kitchen and found water cascading down the fronts of the cabinets by the sink. Within minutes, she feared, the whole main floor of their house would be under a thin layer of slippery suds. Meanwhile, Gran and Grandpa Quirk were both just sitting outside calmly listening to music on the deck. "Oh, oh, oh."

"Gramps!" Penelope shouted, pressing through the back door. "Your dishwater!"

When the twins got outside, Gran fluttered out of Grandpa Quill's palm and hid behind a potted plant. Grandpa Quill leaped up as quickly as he could, considering his roly-poly belly, and muttered, "Aw, pickles, I forgot." He hustled inside, then Molly felt time swoosh backwards. A nanosecond later, the girls were upstairs again, staring at Pen's tiny mini monster – for the second time that night. Finn and Molly were back on the landing, fiddling with the netting from Finn's booby trap. Only Molly realised they'd all been here once before.

"What *is* that?" Finn asked, poking at the fluffy ten-eyed monster.

Molly waited patiently as the rest of the conversation moved on just as she'd remembered it happening the first time. After a few minutes, the sisters were walking back down the stairs to talk to their gran.

Molly peeked into the kitchen as they passed and saw that the sink was filled with soapy water. But this time, Gramps had remembered to turn off the tap before it overflowed. "I guess Mum should have clarified that Gramps needed to clean the kitchen *tonight*," she observed. "He hasn't even started yet. I bet he won't bother doing the dishes until Tuesday."

Pen giggled, because she knew as well as Molly did that this was probably true. "And he's never going to get the plates unglued from the dining-room table."

When the girls got to the deck, Gran – who seemed to get more and more shy with each of the

Quirks' moves – fluttered out of Grandpa Quill's palm and hid behind a potted plant again.

Because she was allergic to the indoors, Gran Quirk had lived much of her adult life in a little house that the Quirks carried with them from town to town. Though she and the girls had always been close, Molly and Pen hadn't got to spend much time with their gran since they'd arrived in Normal. Gran still felt guilty about a little tussle she'd had with the town mayor's cat in the Quirks' last town. It had caused enough of a problem that the family had been forced to move. That was the move that sent them to Normal. Because she knew she was to blame, Gran had spent her first few weeks in Normal hiding out in her house hidden high up in the willow tree.

"Hello, dears," Gran squeaked, fluttering out from behind the pot. She floated over and settled into the space between Penelope's thumb and pinkie finger. "Fun dinner party tonight, I hear?"

"Yeah," Pen said, squinting at her tiny fairy grandmother. "Mum and I were both kind of nervous wrecks before dinner, but everything was fine by the time we had dessert. No major messes."

Grandpa Quill grinned at the girls. "Just the kitchen." He winked and added sleepily, "I suppose I should get on that, eh?" He leaned his head back against his chair and promptly fell asleep. The rewinding – and all the extra pie – had sucked every ounce of energy right out of him.

Gran folded her legs and sat down in Pen's palm. "I sure wish I could have been there. It sounds like this teacher of yours is a nice fellow."

Penelope cupped her palm, making a backrest of fingers for her gran to lean against. Then she and Molly and Gran sat together on the deck and stared up at the dim stars that were slowly creeping out from behind their daytime curtain. The sky was turning blackish blue, but way off in the distance, light was still leaking out of the bottom of the sky, leaving a trail of purple behind.

Gran pulled a tiny biscuit from the pocket of her dress. She split the cookie in thirds and offered a chunk to both girls. The portion wasn't even as big as a crumb, but they both took the offering. Gran could be easily offended, and she'd been known to sulk for several days if someone turned down her food – even if the treat was too small to taste. "Your grandfather brought me a small plate after dinner so I could taste a bit of everything you girls helped your mum make. Delicious."

"Have you ever been to a dinner party, Gran?" Molly asked, turning so she could lean her back against Pen's.

Gran Quirk giggled. Her laugh sounded like coins jingling in someone's pocket. "Of course. I wasn't always this small, you know."

"You weren't always tiny?" Pen asked, surprised. Both girls had just accepted that their grandmother was the size of a Kinder Egg and never asked any questions. Each person's Quirks were their Quirks. No one could explain why some people in their family had the magic they had. Or why Molly had ended up with no Quirk at all.

"No, dear." Gran sighed. "In fact, I was once tall and slender." She fluttered around in the air above Molly and Penelope. "I wasn't born with a Quirk. I married into mine. Didn't you know I was a regular girl until years after I married your grandfather? Years after your mother was born?"

"No!" This was a surprise to both Quirk girls. "How did you get so small? When?" Molly and Pen trailed behind their grandmother as she buzzed into the air and began to snip flowers for a bouquet. Because of Gran's size, Penelope often had a hard time hearing her from a distance.

"Well, one day your grandfather started to have trouble rewinding. He'd tire easily, and sometimes he'd shoot forward in time instead of back. Your great-grandmother Clodagh blamed me." Gran flew right up next to the girls' ears to say, "Your grandpa's mother wasn't a very nice woman, and she had awful, angry powers that soured with age." Gran stopped for a breath and to sniff a tiny, perfect peach rose. "After she'd had her tea, your great-grandmother was a relatively nice lady. But other times, like when we ran out of biscuits, she could be a bit of a witch. The mean kind, not the beautiful sort that floats around in bubbles and grant wishes."

While Gran flitted about, Molly stepped up on

the tightrope. Thanks to Finn's home-made circus set, all three Quirk kids were getting pretty good at both tightrope and trapeze. Niblet even got in on the action when Mrs DeVille wasn't around. In the privacy of their garden, they'd started calling themselves Circus Quirkus – the nickname Nolan had given Penelope after her first turn on the trapeze. They imagined what it would be like if they really were a three-sibling circus. How exciting it would be to travel the country and impress people with their talents, like Vivica and her team did.

Gran continued her story as she buzzed around the garden. "Just days after your grandfather's powers began to weaken, your great-grandmother shrunk me down to the size of a small bird. She was quite sure that if I were smaller I wouldn't be able to get in the way of the other Quirks' powers – and the family's magic would live on."

"Was she right?" Pen asked, her eyes wide. Their home-made trapeze dangled down from a high branch. Pen was hanging upside down from her knees, pumping her arms and swinging through the thick night sky. Her hair hung loose around

her shoulders, brushing the ground as she swung forward and back.

"She was correct." Gran nodded. "Now that I'm small, I don't get in the way of the rest of the family's magic any more. But as often happens when a Quirk gets involved, a few things went wrong. I wasn't always allergic to the indoors."

"So you really *are* allergic to inside?" Molly asked, hopping off the tightrope to stand beside her fairy gran. "I always wondered if maybe you just liked having your own space. It would be kind of cool to live in a real live tree house."

"I don't mind so much," Gran said thoughtfully. "I wish I were still able to get big bear hugs from my family. And every so often, I would like to snuggle up beside your grandfather on the couch to watch TV. And I also miss having afternoon tea with friends, now and again. But I love the gardens I've lived in. It's fun to watch my flowers grow. And I see and hear a lot of interesting things from my perch up in the willow tree." She dropped several clusters of flowers into Molly's waiting arms. Penelope somersaulted off the trapeze and landed on the ground beside her sister. They followed as Gran made her way back towards the deck.

"Actually," Molly said, "that's sort of what we came out here to talk to you about." She hoped they could convince their gran to help them keep an eye on their nosy neighbour. She'd be like their very own tiny spy. "Do you ever see Mrs DeVille doing anything strange?"

Gran kicked off her shoes in Pen's hand and tucked her short legs under her skirt. "Well . . ." Gran giggled again. Threads of yellowish light spread into the garden from the kitchen window. Molly sat on the deck stairs and admired the clusters of pink and red snapdragons, a few hardy roses and several sprigs of fragrant lavender in her arms. "She seems to be an interesting woman."

"Molly and I were wondering," Pen said slowly, "if you wouldn't mind keeping a closer eye on her and letting us know if you see or hear anything we need to worry about."

"What on earth would you need to worry about?" Gran squeaked.

Molly chewed on her lip. "She just seems very curious about us," she said. She looked at Penelope, who nodded. "We think she's trying to blab our secrets to the world."

Gran shook her head. "That's silly. She doesn't know anything about us."

"We're not so sure," Pen said. Neither girl wanted to tell on their brother for snooping in their neighbour's house. But they had to somehow convince their gran that their concerns were justified because Finn had heard Mrs DeVille on the phone with the news reporters. How much more certain could you get? "She's been watching us a lot. We just thought –"

Molly picked up where her sister left off. "Maybe if you could pay a little extra attention to Mrs DeVille and report back if you hear or see anything?" As she adjusted the bouquet in her hand, Molly suddenly felt someone watching them. Though they were tucked safely inside the fence, Molly was sure that a set of eyes was staring at her in the dark. She made the mistake of telling her sister.

Pen's head whipped around. When she spotted a small eye watching them through the hole in the fence, the eye began to grow to the size of a golf ball. Mrs DeVille had been standing in her dying rhododendron bushes, peering at the girls through the black night – and at Gran, whose wings were illuminated by the light pouring out from the kitchen window.

"What have you got there?" Mrs DeVille said, pointing her finger at Pen's palm. "You girls are too old for baby dolls, you know." She thought Gran was a doll! "It's time to grow up and start acting your age. Dolls are for babies."

As she stared at them, Mrs DeVille's eyes continued to grow. Penelope's imagination was making their neighbour's eye bulge out of her head like a tennis ball as she gazed into the dim light of the Quirks' garden. With such a silly and enormous eye, she looked like a cartoon character. Molly shot a look at her sister, who closed her eyes and tried to concentrate on something other than the hole in the fence.

Mrs DeVille grunted. "Someone's been

trampling over in my garden, picking my pansies. I know it's one of you two. Can't keep the two of you straight, so I'll blame you both. Never did trust twins. And with that circus business . . ." Finally, her eye began to shrink. Mrs DeVille reached her crooked fingers up to adjust her glasses. They'd been pushed down the bridge of her nose by the force of her bulging eyeball. "Well? What do you have to say for yourselves? Did I hear that doll talking?" She pointed right at Gran. "What have you got there?"

Penelope's eyes were squeezed closed, but Molly knew that her mind was probably whipping and whirling about with all kinds of crazy thoughts. Suddenly, as Mrs DeVille studied them from behind the fence, Gran Quirk started to grow. Pen's eyes shot open, and she gaped at Gran, who was still sitting in her palm but had quickly become too big to fit comfortably. A moment later, Gran hopped off Pen's palm and stood on the back deck. Her wings began to shrink as her legs and arms were growing and expanding. In a matter of just fifteen seconds, Gran Quirk was taller than Molly and Penelope.

Gran patted at her arms, then wiggled her feet. She marvelled at her full-size body in wonder. "Well, I never . . ." She smiled, then hugged Penelope in a way she had never been able to do before.

Molly's mouth hung open. Her sister's mind had made their gran's body original size again! They'd just been talking about how Gran used to be normal size, and then – *poof!* For a moment, Molly forgot all about Mrs DeVille. She, too, stepped into her gran's arms and cuddled up in her soft, squishy arms.

Mrs DeVille's surprised shrieking cut through the quiet of the evening and the lovely family moment, startling Penelope and scaring Molly. Gran waved at Mrs DeVille, trying to act like a friendly neighbour, but clearly there was no use in trying to pretend that what had just happened was anything other than strange.

Their neighbour's loud gasps were enough to send Penelope's overactive imagination into a panic. In the next moment, Gran began to grow again. Her body stretched and bulged until soon she was more than ten feet tall. She just kept growing bigger and bigger until –

Grandpa grunted in his chair. He awoke with a start. "What's that? Who now?" He looked around sleepily, then jolted up and out of his chair when he saw what had happened. He gaped at Gran, and a smile quickly filled his face. "Rose! My dear!" he cried. But the smile faded when he spotted Mrs DeVille. "Oh, dear," he muttered.

A moment later, Molly felt the air quivering around her, and suddenly they slipped back in time. But they had only popped back ten seconds, to when Gran was normal size. Grandpa Quill looked wistfully at Gran, then he shot time back again. And again.

Because he was so sleepy and had rewound so many times that night already, Grandpa Quill was only able to take them back through small chunks of time. Every time they jumped backwards, Molly had to jog over to his chair and startle him awake. It took six tries, but finally Grandpa landed them far enough back.

For the second time that night, fairy Gran shook her head and said, "That's silly. She doesn't know anything about us."

This time, Molly hurriedly blurted out, "Oh, she sees a lot more than you might think. If you could just keep a closer eye and ear on Mrs DeVille and report back if you hear or see anything that sounds suspicious, that would be awesome." She smiled quickly at Gran, then hurried to push Penelope inside. "OK! Thanks for the flowers and the story, Gran," she said hastily. "Goodnight!"

Even though she knew it was rude to leave in what seemed to be the middle of the conversation, she was eager to get Pen out of the garden before the super-size Gran business could begin anew.

CHAPTER 15

Smushed Squirrel

After the night of their dinner party, and in the days leading up to Bree's weekend away, Penelope's mind worried over ways to keep their neighbour from butting into their business. Molly had told Pen what had happened with Gran, which sent Pen into a panic. From that moment forward, her magic went wild whenever they were home.

One morning, Mrs DeVille's entire garden was filled with slippery, slimy slugs that made it impossible for her to step outside her house. The next afternoon, a soupy fog hung over their whole block. It was so thick that no one could see anything beyond their own home's front windows.

Fortunately, at school, Penelope found she had better control over her Quirk. Without Mrs DeVille near, Pen's mind got to take a little holiday. She threw herself into circus practise and their creepy-crawly science unit and her extra maths practise, and that was usually enough to keep her mind occupied with something other than Mrs DeVille's snooping. But sometimes their sessions with the circus team sent her thoughts flying in other ways.

On Thursday afternoon, the fourth-grade class headed back to the gym for their last practice with Vivica and her team. Most of the fourth graders were still trying to master their tricks, hoping Mr Intihar's class would be selected to perform onstage. Molly was getting really good at the low wire, and Penelope was excelling at the trapeze. Not one kid had figured out how to stay upright on stilts, and only a few of their classmates could juggle. Obviously, everyone was worried about their chances of winning the competition.

When the fourth graders arrived at the gym for their final practice, the fifth graders were just wrapping up their own practice. There were rumours flying around that at least half the fifth-grade class had figured out how to juggle, which had everyone else at Normal Elementary School nervous.

The Quirk girls and the rest of the fourth-grade class gaped at the fifth graders as they finished up. Several of them were expertly juggling three or four coloured balls, one girl was balancing on a rolla-rolla balance board, and another plunged towards them on stilts. They looked like professional circus performers.

"Whoa," Joey muttered. "My clown act is a joke compared to that."

Stella punched him in the shoulder. "Don't forget that we have Penelope. She's our secret weapon."

"Circus Quirkus is good," Nolan agreed quietly. "But the fifth grade is *really* good."

The fifth graders looked proud as they marched

past the fourth graders on their way out of the gym. One of them whispered, "Good luck, losers."

For the next hour, the fourth grade practised harder than ever. A bunch of kids worked on their clown routines together, falling and stumbling and honking their noses to try to get their friends to laugh. Penelope took another turn on the trapeze, then she and Molly and some of the other girls in class tried – and failed – to master the human pyramid they'd been working on all week. Luckily, Stella was tiny enough that when they all crumpled into a heap, no one was hurt since she was on the top.

"Maybe we should tie up the fifth graders and lock them in the gym storage closet," Nolan yelled down from his perch on the trapeze stand. "They can't win if no one can find them." Raade and Joey both laughed as though Nolan were the funniest guy on earth. Their guffawing made them fall off the globe they were hopelessly trying to balance on – again.

"Mr Paulson," Vivica warned. "Please focus on the trapeze bar. We don't want to have any accidents today. Are you ready?"

Penelope, who was now trying her luck with a unicycle, grinned. Nolan was always so boastful, but he was really terrible at the trapeze. He hadn't yet figured out how to do the knee hang. He always fell off after about ten seconds of swinging, then acted like he'd meant to do it.

Nolan wrapped his hands around the trapeze bar, raised it in the air, and yelled, "Ready!"

"Hep!"

As Nolan soared through the air, Penelope found her mind shifting back to the conversation she'd had with Molly the previous week. She knew she was supposed to ignore Nolan, but she just couldn't. How had she described it? Like he was a smushed squirrel . . . the kind of awful creature you can't help but stare at, even though you really don't want to look.

"Oh, no," Penelope muttered as she thought about Nolan . . . and smushed squirrels . . . and Nolan again. Her eyes freaked as she realised what was about to happen, then she slammed them closed. She tried to think of anything other than squirrels, but her head just wouldn't listen. She opened her eyes and squinted up at Nolan. As she watched him swing, Penelope's imagination thrashed inside her head.

Nolan soared over the net. "Ahhh! Woo-hoo!" he yelled as he swung backwards and forwards through the air.

The gym was total chaos as everyone in the fourth grade tried to master the slack line and the juggling corner and the silk ropes. People were shouting and shrieking and whistling. Penelope tried and tried to make her mind stop whirling, but she couldn't. There was just too much going on around her – it was impossible.

Suddenly, as Nolan slipped from the trapeze bar and plummeted down to the net, his backside sprouted a fluffy tail. He shrieked, and a moment later, the tail disappeared as quickly as it had come. If you hadn't been looking, you might not have noticed it at all.

Penelope gasped, then ran from the gym. She was in tears before she even reached the hall. Molly ran after Pen, stopping her just outside the gym doors. "What happened? What's the matter?"

Penelope choked on her tears. "I almost turned Nolan into a squirrel!"

"You *what?*"

"Remember how you told me I have to stop paying attention to him, since he always makes my magic act up? But then I told you I *can't*, because even though he drives me crazy, I just can't stop watching him? Like that time we saw the smushed squirrel? We knew it was going to be gross and everything, but neither of us could tear our eyes away from it?"

"Yeah," Molly said slowly.

"So I kept thinking about him being a squirrel, and then when he fell off the trapeze, he sprouted a tail. A tail, Molly!"

"Did anyone else see it?" Molly asked.

"I don't know!" Pen threw her hands up in the air. "But even if they didn't, I'm worried about what will happen next."

Molly tried to stay calm. "What will happen next?"

"Now I can't get my mind off the idea of Nolan and squirrels," Pen huffed. She lowered her voice to whisper, "What if I accidentally turn Nolan into a *smushed* squirrel?" She stared at Molly, gasping for air. "How do we explain that?"

Molly chewed at her lip. "First of all, that's not going to happen. Second of all, you've got to chill out."

"OK," Pen said, breathing fast. "How am I supposed to do that?"

Before Molly could figure out an answer, Mr Intihar appeared beside them in the hall. "Ladies." He bowed. "May I ask you to please return to the gym? We need to line up for lunch. There's going to be an announcement about next week's circus performance, so I suggest we hustle along."

Pen shot Molly a desperate glance.

"Yeah," Molly said. She smiled at their teacher and dragged her sister back towards the gym doors. "Don't worry," she said, wrapping her arm through Penelope's. "Hopefully some food will keep your mind far, far away from Nolan."

CHAPTER 16 ←

Squirrel Ball

"I'm starving," Izzy announced, flouncing down beside Molly on their usual lunchroom bench a few minutes later. She opened her lunch box and made a face when she looked inside. Molly and Pen could never understand why Izzy was always disappointed by her lunch. She even complained on the days when she got a mini chocolate bar or a package of Oreos. The Quirks never got Oreos. And mini chocolate bars were only for Halloween (even at Halloween, the girls had to come up with very clever hiding places for their choco-late or Grandpa Quill and Niblet would eat it all).

"I seriously hope they pick us to perform with the circus," Stella said, pulling out her water bottle. "We've worked so hard – it would be awe-some if the whole town could watch us. We'd be famous."

Molly nodded and zipped open her lunch box. Inside, she found no surprises. As usual, she had a ham sandwich, an apple, a plastic container of baby carrots and a single cookie. Every day, Molly got the same thing – though she sometimes made a jam sandwich just to shake things up. Penelope's lunch was almost identical to Molly's, but most days she took an orange instead of an apple.

"Pen, did you pack an orange today?" Izzy asked, peeling open her sandwich. She delicately removed the slices of turkey and slapped the but-tered pieces of bread back together before taking a bite. "If it's a big one, can I have half? My mum packed me nothing good."

"Yeah," Penelope muttered, distracted. She was wondering what it would be like to perform in front of the whole town. It would be fun, sure, but she didn't like the idea of the fourth grade in the spotlight. Pen slowly zipped open her lunch bag. It felt heavier than usual, and the bag was large and lumpy. This worried Pen. Her Quirk had been working overtime the last few days, and she had a bad feeling about what she might find inside. She peeked in the bag, and her shoulders slumped.

"That orange is *huge!*" Izzy cried, reaching over to grab it. "Where did you even get this thing?"

Penelope stared at the orange resting on the table in front of Izzy. It was the size of a small football. When she'd packed her fruit that morning, the orange had been totally normal. A regular, baseball-size fruit. But now it was enormous – at least three times the size of her usual orange. Her magical mind had started attacking her fruit now, too. "Great," Pen grouched.

Pen focused every bit of her attention on her sandwich, hoping that the fruit wouldn't continue to grow as it sat in the middle of the table. When Izzy had asked if she could share, Penelope had imagined an enormous orange in her lunch bag, big enough for sharing with everyone . . . and then she'd got exactly what she pictured in her head.

"You don't mind sharing your monster orange, right?" Izzy asked Pen again. Pen shrugged, still focusing all her attention on her sandwich.

"What's with her?" Stella asked, nudging Molly.

Molly locked eyes with Pen. "She's fine. Let's just talk about something else, OK?"

"O-K," Izzy huffed, obviously not convinced.

"Ladies and gentlemen!" Mr Intihar climbed on a milk crate near the peanut-free table and clapped his hands for attention. "Folks, may I have your attention for a few moments, please?"

More than a hundred pairs of eyes turned towards Mr Intihar. Wrappers crinkled and a chair squeaked, but after a few seconds, everyone stopped talking.

Mr Intihar ran his hands through his hair as he spoke. "Students, we've spoken with the Circus of the Dazzling Stars team. And I'm pleased to report that they've come to a decision about which class will be performing for the town of Normal next week."

The lunchroom exploded with conversation as everyone began to speculate about who they would announce as the winner. Izzy crossed her fingers and muttered, "Please please please please . . ."

Stella fiddled with her fringe and looked nervous. "I hope we win," she whined. "I *really* hope he says the fourth grade wins. With Penelope's trapeze skills, we've got to be in the running, right?"

Molly watched her sister, who was holding her breath. Penelope's face was scrunched up. It almost looked like she was going to cry. "You OK?" Molly asked, poking her twin in the side.

"I just wish we could *all* perform," Pen

whispered, so quietly that Molly could scarcely hear her over the din of conversation. "Everyone's worked so hard, and it doesn't seem fair that some kids get to perform in front of an audience and others don't. It would be so much more fun that way."

Mr Intihar clapped his hands for attention again. The lunchroom noise simmered to a low boil of quiet muttering. Pen and Molly stared at Mr Intihar, along with everyone else. Once again, Penelope had her face squished up tight, as though she was focusing all her energy on the announcement.

"We have good news for all of you," Mr Intihar shouted. "The circus team has decided that *every* class deserves a chance at the spotlight – you've all worked very hard. So each of Normal's six classrooms will be performing next week, in front of all your parents, grandparents, neighbours, and friends. Kindergarten through to fifth grade!"

The lunchroom exploded with applause. Penelope's eyes popped open. "We all win?" she asked. "Everyone gets to perform during the circus?"

"That's what he said," said Molly. "I guess you got your wish."

Penelope's eyes widened. "Do you think that's what he was going to say? Or do you think somehow I . . ." She trailed off.

"I guess we'll never know," said Molly, grinning.

Everyone chatted excitedly until the end of lunch. As they rushed out to the playground for break-time, Pen felt better than she had all week. The whole time they played football on the field, Penelope was practically glowing. Molly high-fived her. "You're totally going to get to show off your crazy trapeze skills."

"So will a lot of people," Penelope said gleefully. She broke away from her sister to chase a stray ball that had rolled to the very back of the football field. That's when she saw something that made her good mood go sour. In the matted-down dirt by the maintenance shed, a squirrel was spinning in circles, as though it didn't know how to work its tiny legs. The creature's fur was all dirty and gross, and its fluffy tail was flicking around in the air. Penelope skidded to a stop and stared at the squirrel. The squirrel stopped spinning and planted its four feet on the

ground. Still as a statue, the little animal stared right back at Penelope.

The ball lay unmoving a few tiny steps away from where Pen and the squirrel stood in a stand-off. Penelope knew she could just tiptoe around the squirrel and kick the ball back into the game. But she was stuck. Someone yelled out, "Hey, Pen, kick it here!"

Still, Penelope couldn't move. She leaned down to peer at the squirrel more closely. Something about the creature's tiny face looked familiar. "Nolan?" she asked aloud. "Did you turn into a squirrel?"

The squirrel said nothing. Penelope shook her head, worried that she'd been thinking about Nolan and squirrels *again*.

Finally, Pen made a timid move towards the ball. The squirrel took a few quick steps towards the ball, too, as though it was eager to join the fourth graders' game. It chittered and chattered at her, almost like it was trying to tell her something. Penelope watched, fascinated, when the squirrel pounced to stand on the football. Pen was almost sure the little creature stuck its tongue out at her. "Nolan? Is that you?" Penelope asked quietly. This was just the sort of thing that would send the Quirks packing. Turning a classmate into a squirrel wasn't exactly something you could make people forget. Mrs DeVille was one kind of trouble. But this . . . *this* was *terrible*.

The squirrel tilted its head, its beady eyes staring at Penelope. Then, with a flick of its tail, the squirrel hopped off the ball and dashed into the bushes at the edge of the field. Moments later, Nolan Paulson came running onto the field. He was yelling, "Hey, Circus Quirkus! The ball! Are you going to kick it back today, or next week?"

Nolan ran up to Penelope, stuck his tongue out at her, and dribbled the ball back. As she hustled to rejoin the game, Penelope realised that, in all their weeks in Normal, she had never before been so happy to see Nolan Paulson.

Hiccup House

"Kids, I'm off! Come give me kisses!" Bree stood by the front door of the Quirks' house the next afternoon. The weekend of her girls' getaway had arrived. A rumpled overnight bag stood to attention by her side.

Finn charged over and held his mum in a giant, sticky hug. Each of his fingertips was wrapped in a ripped piece of a fruit roll. His fingers looked like bloody stumps. After Finn stepped out of his hug, Penelope relaxed into her mother's arms.

Finally – reluctantly – Molly squeezed her mother close and wished her a fun weekend. "Oh, it will be fun," Bree said cheerfully. "I just hope you kids do OK here without me. You will, won't you? Promise me." She focused on her children, looking them each in the eye.

Molly said nothing, but both Penelope and Finn promised.

"Should I have George come over to check on you tomorrow?" Bree asked, just as a car rolled up in front of the Quirks' house. Someone honked the horn, two quick short blasts. "I could have him come over and make sure everything's OK. See if you need anything."

"Mr Intihar?" Molly asked, wrinkling her nose.

"No, sirree," Grandpa Quill chimed in. "I'm a perfectly capable adult. We will be abso*toot*ly fine here." He pointed a finger in the air, as if to punctuate his point.

"All right, then," Bree said softly, blowing them all kisses one last time. "I'll see you on Sunday morning."

As soon as she was gone, Grandpa grabbed

a bag of salt-and-vinegar crisps from the cupboard and settled down on the couch. He propped his feet up on a pile of pillows, threw his dirty socks across the room, and turned on the television. "Now, this is the life," he muttered. He peeled open two individual packets of ketchup. Then Grandpa Quill carefully drizzled a blob of ketchup on each crisp before popping a whole messy handful into his mouth.

Finn, Molly and Penelope stood in a line in the front hall, watching Grandpa Quill make a mess of the couch and his shirt. "What now?" Finn asked finally. He licked the fruit rolls on his fingers, nibbling off each finger cast. "Should we set up some booby traps outside, just in case?"

"It probably can't hurt," Penelope agreed. "What if Mrs DeVille's reporter friends come snooping around this weekend while Mum's gone?"

"What reporter friends?" Grandpa Quill asked through a mouthful of crisps. He turned around on the couch so he could look at the three kids, who were still standing in a line in the hall. Several chunks of salty crisps hung off his moustache. There was a streak of ketchup shooting across his ruddy cheek.

"I guess we might as well fill Gramps in," Molly said reluctantly. Now that their mum had actually gone, she wasn't feeling quite as confident that they could handle Mrs DeVille on their own. "We might need Gramps's help later, if anything happens."

"Help? Magic help?" Grandpa Quill asked, rubbing his hands together. "Ooh-hoo! I love doing magic help." He licked his fingers, one by one, with a loud slurp.

Molly filled him in on all the times they'd seen Mrs DeVille snooping. Then she told him what Finn had heard when he was poking around in her house. "We think she's trying to expose our secrets to everyone in Normal. She seems really interested in our Quirks, and I think she's on to something. We're pretty sure she's trying to get a reporter over here to film us, and we need to keep them from seeing anything."

Grandpa pounded his hands on the couch scatter cushions. He was suddenly full of energy. "Tell me what we're doing! What's the plan, Stan?" He rolled up the top of the crisp bag and tucked it under a scatter cushion on the couch. Then he began to stand up. But suddenly, his eyes widened, he sat back down, and his face went red.

Molly was the first to realise what was happening. "Hiccups!" she cried, realising that her grandpa was holding his breath. "Gramps, did you get the hiccups from eating your crisps and ketchup too fast?"

Grandpa said nothing. His answer came in the form of a loud, shrieking hic-*cup*. Suddenly, the Quirks were all bounced back in time. They'd skipped back about a minute. Once again, Finn asked, "What now?"

Hiccup!

Then time bounced and crashed again, sending them all forward to the moment right after Grandpa said, "Magic help? Ooh-hoo!"

Hiccup!

Back they went, then forward. Forward, back. This is what happened whenever Grandpa Quill got the hiccups. For the rest of the world, hiccups are no big deal. They are annoying, sure, and sometimes you heard about people who got hiccups for months on end. There was even the girl who'd had hiccups for ten years, or something like that. Molly had read about her in a record book at their last school. But even that was nothing compared to what happened when Grandpa Quill got the hiccups. Molly was pretty sure no one else's hiccups made time bump and crash back and forth the way Grandpa Quill's did.

"Gramps!" Molly said, reaching for him between time flips. She and Grandpa were the only two people who realised they were doing a time-dance. "Lean over and drink some water upside down."

But before he could get to the kitchen to fill a cup, they all bumped back again.

Hiccup!

Grandpa covered his mouth with his hand, then he held his breath. He tried everything he could to make the hiccups stop, but it was no use. They just kept skidding from moment to moment as the hiccups came faster and faster.

Hiccup!

Time skipped forward once again, and Molly knew they'd bumped ahead more than a few seconds this time, since she and Finn were suddenly in the upstairs hall. But she had no idea how far in the future they'd landed. She and her brother both looked around curiously. Though Finn had no idea time was skittering around the way it was, Molly knew he must be feeling shaken and silly and a little dizzy. After each hiccup, it always took a moment or two for the people nearby to figure out where they were and what exactly was happening.

Molly stared around, trying to get her bearings. Suddenly, she heard a rapping sound on her bedroom window. It made Molly's stomach turn nervously. Someone was knocking on her window! Molly crouched down and made her way towards her bedroom.

Gran was fluttering on the other side of the glass, waving at her. Molly slid open the window and peered out. "Molly!" Gran said urgently. She pointed down at the side garden. Molly looked out and saw a news van rolling up to the kerb in front of Mrs DeVille's house. "You told me to keep an eye and an ear on Mrs DeVille. Well, I did and she's –"

Hiccup!

"No!" Molly cried, realising Grandpa's hiccup had sent them back again. She hadn't had enough time to hear what Gran had to say and to see what exactly was happening outside. Now they were back in the front hall, standing in front of Grandpa and his open bag of crisps again.

Grandpa was hastily stuffing a handful of crisps into his mouth, trying to get his hiccups to just calm down. Five seconds passed, then ten. When no one said anything, Finn asked, "Why are we all just standing here?" He looked around, his mouth hanging open. He whispered, "What's going on? Why so quiet?" He sucked on the last of his fruit rolls.

After fifteen seconds passed without another hiccup, Molly breathed a sigh of relief. "Gone!" Grandpa said proudly, wiping the salt off his hands on to his trousers.

Penelope and Finn looked around curiously. "Did you have the hiccups?" Finn asked. "Did we flip around in time?" He looked to Molly for an answer.

"Yes," Molly said in a rush. "And when we hopped forward, I saw something!"

"What kind of something?" Pen asked. She twisted at a curl behind her left ear and looked around, as though something might pop out from behind their overstuffed armchair.

"The reporters are coming," Molly said hurriedly. "When we hopped forward, Gran was knocking at our bedroom window to tell us something. And there was a news van pulling up out front! I'm absolutely sure the reporters are on their way here now."

"Whoa," Grandpa Quill said, tucking his bag of crisps under the cushion again. "I popped us forward that far into the future? Pretty cool. That hasn't happened for a long time." He yawned hugely and slumped back against the couch cushions.

Molly nodded. "Yeah, it is cool. Because this gives us a head start! We know the reporters are coming, and now we're one step ahead of them!" Molly beamed. "It's time to get Mrs DeVille and her team of snoops off our backs for good!"

CHAPTER 18

A Thousand Eyes

Molly Quirk had felt like a hero only once before in her life. At Normal Night a couple of weeks earlier, Molly's ideas and courage had helped her family save the day when things were going horribly wrong. Now she had a chance to do it again. But suddenly Molly didn't feel much like being a hero. She felt like crawling upstairs, closing the door to her bedroom, and curling up under the bed with Niblet.

Because the honest truth was, Molly was scared.

Strangers were outside, trying to get a glimpse of the Quirks' secrets. And no one could know about their secrets.

Pen walked over to stand beside the couch, where Grandpa Quill had collapsed after his hiccups. "He's totally out," Pen said, waving one of Grandpa's own dirty socks under his nose to try to wake him.

Finn leaped on to the couch and squirted a blob of ketchup on his finger. Then he drew a wet, red beard on Grandpa's face. "Ketchup, Gramps. Wakey-wakey. Yum yum." But Grandpa Quill barely moved.

"He's exhausted from the hiccups," Molly guessed. "Too much rewinding. He must be totally wiped out. We're going to have to make it the rest of the night without him or his Quirk."

"No do-overs?" Pen asked. She twisted at the curl behind her ear again.

Molly poked at Grandpa Quill. He grunted and groaned, then rolled on to his side and let out a huge, rumbling snore. It was obvious he was going to be asleep for hours. "No more of Grandpa's do-overs tonight."

Suddenly, the sound of car doors slamming came from the street out front. Loud voices carried through the closed windows in the Quirks' house. Penelope gasped. "They're here!"

Molly took a deep breath, poked her face between the closed curtains, and peeked out of the front window. A guy wearing a Channel One vest was unloading a ladder from his van. Behind Mr Channel One, there was a lady holding a video camera and a big microphone. Mrs DeVille's reporter friends had finally come to get their footage of the Quirks' carefully guarded secrets.

"It's just you, me and Finn versus whoever's out there."

"Don't forget about Gran!" Finn piped in.

Molly nodded. "Right. And Gran. It's time for us to make sure Mrs DeVille knows she should not mess with the Quirks. She needs to mind her own business from now on." Molly studied her sister's and brother's serious expressions over Grandpa Quill's sleeping form.

Pen and Finn stared at Molly blankly. "How do we do that?" Finn asked finally.

"We need to throw them off our trail, for good," Molly said as Grandpa Quill honked out a huge snore. Molly made her way into the front hall, and her siblings trailed behind her. "We need to find some way to get Mrs DeVille to stop *wondering* so much. And we need to convince those reporters that they came all the way out here with their big fancy cameras for nothing." Molly stopped walking so suddenly that Penelope and Finn both crashed into her. She righted herself, then spun around to face her siblings.

"What if we set up some booby traps outside?" Finn suggested. "I'll play Captain Invisible and get it all ready. We'll catch 'em and lock up the reporters and Mrs DeVille until they leave us alone. They'll be our prisoners for ever." Finn squirmed excitedly. "I can be the pirate captain and make them walk the plank! *Arrr!*"

Molly knew that her brother didn't get just how serious the situation was. It wasn't like they were playing tag or pirates with neighbourhood friends. These were *adults*. Sneaky peeky adults who could get the Quirks kicked out of Normal – unless someone could figure out some way to make them go away once and for all.

Molly chewed at her lip, thinking. She spoke aloud as she mused over the options. "We could do booby traps, but we can't hold them prisoner." Finn looked so disappointed that Molly added, "Your booby traps were awesome for inside the house, Finn. When we were worried someone might come in to take Niblet, you saved the day."

"So what are we supposed to do tonight, then?" Pen asked her sister. "Just hide out in here and hope they go away?"

"We definitely could do that, too," Molly agreed. "But they'll just keep coming back. It's not like Mrs DeVille's going to back off anytime soon. We need to find some way to make the reporters go away without finding out the truth about us. But how?"

Pen watched Molly as she was thinking. Suddenly, an illustrated thought bubble popped into the air over Molly's head. A big question mark materialised in the centre of the thought bubble. Molly grimaced at her sister. "That's not helping."

"Sorry," Pen said. "It's just . . . I can tell you're thinking so hard."

Molly's eyes opened wide, and the question mark above her turned into an exclamation point. "I have an idea!"

"I knew it!" Pen exclaimed. The thought bubble over Molly's head disappeared in a puff of steam. "What is it?"

Molly beamed. "Who's up for a little circus action?"

"I'm always up for circus stuff," Finn said. "But how's that going to help us?"

"We'll give those reporters something to see, all right," Molly said. "But the only footage they're going to get is of our very own Circus Quirkus."

Finn and Penelope looked stumped.

"We'll perform for them!" Molly cried.

"Circus tricks?" Penelope asked slowly. "You think *circus tricks* are going to get them to go away?"

Molly's shoulders slumped. "It's worth a shot, right?" Penelope and Finn did not look convinced. "We have to come up with something that will take the attention away from all the other stuff they could see – like Gran, Niblet, Finn going invisible, Penelope's creative imagination . . ." Molly peeked out of the back door, then eased it open. No one was there yet, but Molly knew it was just a matter of time. "Let's put on a show for them."

Gran Quirk fluttered over to the kids on the deck. From behind a potted plant she squeaked, "*Psst.*"

"Gran!" Molly exclaimed.

"There are reporters in the front garden," Gran said hurriedly. "I overheard Mrs DeVille talking to them and tried to warn you, but –"

"We know," Molly said, cutting her off. "You *did* warn us. Now we need your help."

"Certainly," Gran said. "I'm happy to do whatever you need me to do."

For the next few minutes, Gran went to work stringing twinkling Christmas lights all around the garden. Her wings were powerful and she worked fast. Soon the garden was aglow with colour, making it look like a magical circus wonderland. The trapeze was lit from above, and the tightrope from below. There was a glowing ring of lights that would be perfect for Finn's juggling exhibition.

While Gran decorated, Molly, Finn and Penelope stretched their muscles and put on some of Grandpa Quill's football jerseys. "It's the closest thing we've got to costumes," Molly explained. "They're not perfect, but at least we look like a team! Sort of . . ."

Penelope squeezed her eyes shut, and in the next instant the jerseys all transformed. What had been plain old football jerseys were now sparkling costumes with the words CIRCUS QUIRKUS emblazoned on the back.

"Neat," Finn said, admiring his outfit. "I'm glowy." A moment later, the sparkles faded and the jerseys morphed back into regular jerseys again.

"Sorry," Pen said. "I can't make the magic last long enough."

Molly shrugged. "It's OK. The jerseys work. But we should have Gran make us some costumes. For next time."

"I already did!" Gran hooted as she fluttered back to the deck. "I've been working on them for the past week. I was going to surprise you for your big circus performance at the school." She tugged at a basket that was tucked under the Adirondack chair. "But there's no time like the present." Tiny knitting needles and a miniature sewing kit spilled out of the basket and scattered across the deck. Finn leaned down to help her. He tugged three glittery, golden uniforms out of the basket and tossed one to each of his sisters. All three Quirk kids slipped on their homemade Circus Quirkus suits.

"These are beautiful, Gran!" Penelope said, spinning around. "Thank you!"

A flash illuminated the garden, and Gran fluttered out of view again. "There they are!" The man in the Channel One vest was setting up a ladder on the other side of the fence. He climbed up it and peered over the tall fence to wave at the Quirks. "Do something unbelievable for us, kids. Let's see what you've got!"

Molly and Penelope both stood in the backyard, shielding their eyes from the bright news camera lights. Meanwhile, Finn danced around like a lunatic. His suit glowed and twinkled as he spun and captured all the attention.

"With all those cameras and lights, it feels like there are a thousand eyes watching us," Penelope observed, twisting nervously at one of her curls as she stepped into the shadows by the house.

Molly looked over at the fence, where hundreds of tiny eyes were suddenly embedded in the fence posts. Penelope's mind had made them appear just below the reporters who were peering over the fence at their crazy brother. "Don't think about that," Molly cautioned. "Pen, all you need to do is think about the trapeze. You are a trapeze superstar. Let's show these reporters something amazing, and then hopefully they'll be satisfied and go away!"

All the tiny eyes faded into plain wood fence again, and Penelope breathed out a sigh of relief. Pen gazed at the group of people who were staring at them from their ladder perches. "I don't see Mrs DeVille anywhere."

Just as she said that, Mrs DeVille's face peeked out from behind the curtain in her upstairs window. She had her binoculars pressed to her eyes, and she was staring down into the Quirks' garden. Molly and Pen noticed her at the same time. Suddenly, the glassy fronts of the binocular lenses turned into huge, glowing eyeballs. The binoculars blinked at the girls and continued to stare right at them.

One of the reporters hollered, "Come on, kids! We don't have all night. Let's see some of this crazy stuff your neighbour told us about. Get on with it!"

As Pen and Molly stood in the garden, there was a scuffle at the back door. Both girls turned and gasped at the same time. "Niblet!" Pen said in a hushed voice. "What are you doing out here?"

CHAPTER 19

Circus Quirkus

Niblet peeked around the edge of the door. He goggled at the reporters and blinked. He had a blankie wrapped around his shoulders, and when he shrugged it off, Molly giggled. "You're wearing your circus tutu again!"

Niblet spun around just inside the door to the house, modelling his outfit. He'd also found a pair of fluffy bunny earmuffs, and a tartan scarf was wrapped jauntily around his neck. "He's so cute," Pen cooed. Then she jumped up and down. "Molly!

What if Niblet joined Circus Quirkus tonight, too? He's been practising his juggling and his mime routine so hard. He deserves a chance to perform. Don't you think?"

Molly eyed her sister suspiciously. "How are we going to explain a juggling monster?"

Penelope thought for a moment, then exclaimed, "He could pretend to be a giant puppet! If we were standing behind him when he did his thing, it would look like we were making him move." She looked at Niblet. "You could do that, right, buddy?

Pretend to be a stuffed animal, like Molly's piggy? Just don't move a muscle unless one of us is near you. It can be our little secret."

Niblet nodded eagerly.

"OK," Molly agreed. "Let's carry him and prop him up until it's time." Pen and Molly clumsily carried Niblet around. The monster slumped in a lawn chair, looking an awful lot like a huge stuffed animal who'd been stuck playing a game of dressing-up. Finn waved at their monster, then he began to dance again.

"I hope this gets interesting soon," the lady with the video camera grumbled. "So far, all I've got on camera is a couple of kids in funny costumes with a ratty-looking stuffed animal."

That's when Penelope grabbed her trapeze bar confidently. Molly and the reporters all watched as Pen swung back and forth under the old oak tree. She pulled her knees up to do a knee hang. The news people gathered around the fence *ooh*-ed and *ahh*-ed, focusing their cameras on Pen.

"She's flying!" one of the reporters yelled. "Look at her go!"

As Penelope soared through the air, Finn stood behind Niblet and tickled him. Niblet flailed and squirmed about, looking just like a floppy puppet. The reporters all laughed and pointed. Niblet did exactly what he was supposed to do, slumping over like a furry lump every time Finn stepped away from his side.

After a few minutes, Finn jogged towards the brightly lit juggling ring. Gran zipped through the shadowed space against the fence and tossed Finn *one*, *two*, *three* apples from the apple tree on the other side of the house. Finn tossed the apples into the air and juggled them. Again, the reporters seemed impressed. "So young!" one of them observed, training a camera on Finn. "And already such a skilled juggler."

Finn walked towards Niblet as he juggled the apples higher and higher. Molly moved to stand behind their monster just as Finn tossed the apples towards them. Niblet caught them and juggled like a pro. Molly stood behind their monster the whole time and moved her arms with his, making it look like she was manning him like a puppet. After a few seconds, Niblet tossed the apples back to Finn, then slumped down in his chair again, playing the part of a stuffed animal perfectly.

The guy in the vest turned to the lady with the camera and said, "Now, that's neat. I bet that stuffed animal is the weird pet their neighbour was talking about. The squishy stuffed guy is part of the kids' routine. Mrs DeVille was probably just looking for a story angle."

Molly giggled, then stepped up on the tight-rope. She began to walk across it, holding her arms out to her sides. When she got to the middle of the rope, she did a cartwheel and landed back on her feet again. The reporters cheered.

Next, the Quirks got ready to do the trick they'd been working on for the last few days. First, Finn threw one of his apples to Penelope. She caught it with her hands as she dangled by her knees and swung through the air on the trapeze bar. Gran fluttered by with another apple, and Finn tossed it up in the air with the other two.

Meanwhile, Pen tossed the apple to Molly. Molly caught the apple in one hand. She teetered unsteadily on the tightrope, but then she righted herself again. Carefully, she took the apple and balanced it on her head.

A moment later, Finn tossed a second apple to Pen. Then Pen tossed it to Molly. Molly stacked the second apple on top of the first. Both apples were balanced on her head, and Molly was still walking along the tightrope.

The Quirk kids did this a third time, with Gran delivering a replacement apple each time. But this time, when Pen tossed the apple to Molly, Molly tossed it back. Pen swung through the air, back and forth, then tossed the apple to Finn. Finn caught it - and didn't even have to stop juggling! He grinned. It was the first time their routine had really worked. Both Molly and Finn suspected that Penelope's magical mind had something to do with it all working out as it should.

Several of the news people whooped. "This really is something!" one of them noted. "These kids have a mini circus ring in their garden. This is a great angle for our story about the Circus of the Dazzling Stars' performance next week!"

The lady with the camera cheered. "Yes! We can show some footage of these kids practising in their garden, then we'll talk about how the students at Normal Elementary have been learning circus tricks in gym class. It's the perfect story for the nightly news! And now we've got an amazing video to show with it!"

The reporters seemed pleased with what they'd seen. They began to climb back down their ladders. "Thanks for the show, kids," the vest guy called out. "And thank your neighbour for letting us know about this. It really is some crazy cool stuff."

Molly, Pen, Finn, Gran and Niblet all watched as the news reporters disappeared into their vans and cars. When everyone had gone, Pen somersaulted off the trapeze, Molly jumped off the tightrope, and Finn practised balancing his apples on his head. The sound of silence was comforting.

After a moment, Molly high-fived her brother and sister. "We did it! They're gone!"

Penelope turned to Niblet. "Good job, pal. You aced it! But now we should get you inside before you freeze to death." Niblet shivered as he hustled up the stairs to the warmth of the house.

Gran zipped down from her house in the willow tree. "That was quite a show," she said.

"Thanks," Molly said, smiling. Gran landed on Penelope's shoulder and cuddled up inside Pen's hair. "We couldn't have done it without you."

Before the Quirks could celebrate any more, Mrs DeVille's voice carried through the silence of the evening. "Now, where on earth did those reporters go?"

CHAPTER 20

The Juggler

The kids and Gran looked over at the fence and saw that Mrs DeVille was in her regular spot - peeking through the hole that gave her a view into the Quirks' garden.

Molly walked over to the fence and said, "The reporters are gone."

"Gone? Already?"

"Mrs DeVille," Molly said, her voice catching. She was still scared of their neighbour. "I know you don't like us," she said slowly.

Mrs DeVille's eyeball widened behind the hole in the fence. "Who said that?"

Molly pulled her eyebrows together. "You did." She swallowed, then added, "Ma'am."

"I said I think you're odd," Mrs DeVille said crossly. "And I don't like some of the things you do – like picking my flowers. But I never said I don't like *you*. I don't even know you."

"Oh," Molly said. "But you said you thought we had something to hide . . . and then you've been so busy snooping on us that –"

Mrs DeVille cut her off. "Pish posh," she said. "I can snoop all I want. You're my neighbours. Neighbours keep an eye on each other. It's our job."

Molly wasn't sure what she could say to that, so she said nothing at all.

"I do think you're odd folks," Mrs DeVille said gruffly. "And kids make me sneeze. But that doesn't mean I dislike you." She grunted and stared at Molly through the hole in the fence. "Since the day you moved in, I've had a feeling you were hiding something. At first, I thought you had some horrible secret." Molly held her breath, waiting

for Mrs DeVille to continue. Here it was . . . the moment they'd been worried about. How much did Mrs DeVille know about them? Was it time to move again?

Mrs DeVille sounded excited when she said, "But now I know you've been hiding pure talent! I enjoy watching your little circus business out of the window. That's why I had the news people come out. I thought they should see it, too."

"Wait," Molly said, confused. Penelope had come to stand behind her, with Gran still hidden under the cover of her curls. Finn wandered over and held Molly's hand. "You called the news reporters because of our garden circus? Because of Circus Quirkus?"

"Of course," Mrs DeVille said. "It's really something special. I told them my neighbour kids had a big surprise over here, and that they ought to come and get some footage. It's taken them long enough, too. A garden circus is a pretty neat idea, if you ask me. More people should appreciate circus arts."

"You like the circus, Mrs DeVille?" Penelope piped up quietly from behind Molly.

Mrs DeVille narrowed her eye and admitted, "I might." She took a deep breath, then added, "In fact, many years ago, I was something of a circus performer myself."

"You were?" Finn asked. He blew a big bubble with his gum, then sucked it back into his mouth.

"I was," Mrs DeVille said. "I was a juggler, just like you, kid. Travelled around with an incredible circus act for many years. I tell you, that was a collection of strange folks. Strange – and wonderful." She chuckled. "Those were good times, some of the best years of my life. But then it came time to grow up and give up."

"But you didn't want to give up juggling?" Molly asked.

"Not one bit," Mrs DeVille said wistfully. "I would have stayed with that circus for years – we were a family of lovable freaks – but my parents told me it was time to grow up and act my age. Get married. Make a home for a family of my own." She shrugged. "Not that that ever happened. Never did like kids."

"That's so sad," Pen mused.

Again, Finn blew a bubble with his gum. This time, the bubble grew and grew until it finally popped in a big sticky mess all over his face. Finn plucked the tiny wad of gum from his mouth and began to dab it on the sticky chunks of gum that were stuck to his cheeks. With the gum removed, Finn's body faded out of view. Right in front of Mrs DeVille.

Mrs DeVille gasped. "How'd you do that?" she asked, her eye scanning the space around Molly and Penelope, searching for Finn. "I've watched you do that before, and I can't figure out how you do your disappearing act. Is it some sort of optical illusion?"

"Uh-oh." Finn hid behind his sisters and jammed the wad of gum back in his mouth. His body came back into view again.

"That's just amazing," Mrs DeVille said. "Your act would be a dream come true for any professional circus, you know. Have you told the Circus of the Dazzling Stars about what you can do?"

Finn shook his head. "No."

"And we'd rather keep Finn's, um, *tricks* private," Molly added. "If you don't mind."

"Absolutely. I understand completely. Your secret is safe with me. No circus performer needs to reveal the hidden bits of their act, unless they want to." Mrs DeVille's eye blinked – Molly was pretty sure she'd just winked at them. All of a sudden, their crabby old neighbour didn't seem quite as bad as she had in the past. "I've been hiding my own juggling talents for years. Though I can't say I don't regret it."

"You should start juggling again," Finn said. "It would be cool if you could teach me some stuff. I can only juggle three little things, and I really want to learn how to juggle fire."

Mrs DeVille blinked quickly, and Molly noticed that tears were welling up in her eye. "I suppose I could show you a few things." She sniffed noisily, and stepped back from the fence to blow her nose. "You know, my best friend, Joyce, lived in your house for years. She moved out a few months ago. I wouldn't mind having someone to spend some time with."

Molly and Penelope looked at each other. Mrs DeVille was full of surprises.

"Wanna watch TV together someday?" Finn said eagerly. "I love that circus show you sometimes have on."

Molly slugged him. "Finn," she whispered. "You can't tell her you've been in her house. You're not supposed to know what shows she watches."

Mrs DeVille cleared her throat and said, "I guess that would be fine."

"You want to try out our trapeze, too?" Finn asked. "You can come over anytime to play."

Mrs DeVille laughed. It was the first time any of the Quirks had heard their neighbour sound happy. Her laugh was kind of scary, actually. Molly figured that Mrs DeVille probably didn't laugh that often, so her laugh muscles were maybe a little rusty. "I'm not cut out for trapeze. Bad hip. But if you wanted me to sit and have some tea and watch while you kids do your tricks, that would be fine, too."

Penelope felt Gran flutter her wings under the cover of Pen's hair. Gran's tiny little wings tickled

Pen's neck. "I'd be happy to join you for tea," Gran called out hopefully.

"What's that?" Mrs DeVille asked, her eye roving around searching for the source of Gran's voice. "Speak up. I can't hear you whispering!"

"I said . . ." Gran flew out from behind the curtain of Pen's hair. "I'd be happy to join you for a spot of tea, if you'd be willing."

Mrs DeVille pulled off her glasses and rubbed at her eye. In the space of those few seconds, while Mrs DeVille's attention was on her glasses, Gran began to grow. Molly peeked at her sister and saw that Pen's eyes were closed tight. She was wearing her concentration face. Her lips were all bunched up, and her face was twisted tight. Every ounce of her energy was focused on Gran. By the time Mrs DeVille placed her glasses back on the bridge of her nose, Gran Quirk had grown to be full size. "Now, where on earth did you come from?" Mrs DeVille snapped.

Gran beamed at Penelope. Then she turned to face Mrs DeVille. "I'm Rose," Gran said, waving.

"I'd love to sit with you for a spot of tea anytime, if you'd be willing."

Mrs DeVille's eye narrowed, then she said, "That would be fine."

Molly knew this would surely end badly. There was no way Penelope could keep Gran full size for ever. Somehow she'd managed to make Gran grow at the perfect moment, but it couldn't last. Eventually Mrs DeVille would discover that Gran was a fairy. When she discovered that truth, Mrs DeVille would begin to see the Quirks for what they really were – magical misfits. Strange . . . and stuffed with secrets.

"I miss having afternoon tea with friends," Gran said, rubbing her hands together enthusiastically. "We could make it a regular thing, if you don't mind."

Mrs DeVille's voice caught in her throat as she said, "I wouldn't mind at all. It's just the thing I've been missing since Joyce left." Mrs DeVille sniffled – Molly realised she was crying happy tears – and pulled her glasses off again. She looked down at the ground on her side of the fence.

In that moment, Gran began to shrink again. She shrivelled up just as quickly as she'd grown. By the time Mrs DeVille had dropped her glasses back on to the bridge of her nose again, Gran had snapped back to miniature. "Oh!" Gran gasped in her tiny voice. She patted at the folds of her skirt. "Oh, my."

Mrs DeVille's eyes grew wide. "Rose?" she asked, staring at her. "Rose?!" Her startled voice carried through the night. She was beginning to sound hysterical.

"Yes, it's still me," Gran said sadly, in the loudest voice she could manage. "Unfortunately, I'm a little different from most other women you might know." She flapped her wings and held her hands out at her sides.

The Quirk kids all held their breath.

After a moment, Gran spoke timidly to say, "This is who I am. Different. A tad smaller than other people. But I meant what I said. We can still have tea, if you don't mind spending time with a fairy."

Mrs DeVille blinked. Then she coughed. Her breaths grew shorter and shallower. After a long pause, she sighed. "I don't suppose it really matters at all, does it?" She whistled. "It's a bit different from what I'm used to – Joyce isn't exactly a tiny woman – but a friend is a friend, and tea is tea. I couldn't really care less what you look like, I suppose."

Molly and Penelope glanced at each other. "Mrs DeVille?" Molly said. "Most people don't know about Gran –"

"I can imagine not," Mrs DeVille interrupted.

She laughed, and it sounded crackly and awkward again. "It's not often people see a woman the size of a bird."

"Will you . . . tell people about her?" Penelope wondered.

"I don't see any reason to do that," Mrs DeVille said crossly. "Are you going to tell this whole stinking town about my juggling?"

"Not if you don't want us to," Finn promised. "We like secrets."

Molly added, "But I think you should be proud of your juggling. Not many people were professional circus jugglers. It's cool that you have something that makes you so unique."

Mrs DeVille thought for a moment. "Huh. You make a good point, and it's one to consider." She sniffed, then fixed her eyeball on Finn. "But first, kid, let's juggle. We'll see if these old arms still have the magic touch."

CHAPTER 21
The Flying Squirrels

A few nights later, almost everyone in Normal crowded into the elementary school gym. Portable tiers of benches had been set up along the walls. The oval ring where the circus troupe did all their tricks was squeezed into the middle of everything. Neon lights flashed, and music blasted out of speakers. Molly, Penelope and the rest of the fourth-grade class huddled nervously behind the trapeze net, waiting for their big moment.

The kindergartners and first graders had

performed their circus acts first. Molly and Pen were able to sit on the benches with their mum and Grandpa Quill while Finn juggled alongside some of his classmates. The little kids were extra-cute, since they all fell and tumbled a lot, looking more like silly clowns than anything. The second and third graders had gone next, and they'd also been a big hit. A few of the third-grade boys got tangled up in the silk ropes during their performance, and they captured most of the attention from the audience. Now it was the fourth and fifth graders' turn to sail into the centre ring and showcase everything they'd learned from Vivica and her team in the last couple of weeks.

"I'm so proud of all of you," Mr Intihar said, standing in front of his class. "Are you ready to show off a bit?"

"Yes!" the class cried.

"Are you sure?" Mr Intihar asked again.

"Yes!" The whole fourth-grade class went crazy, jumping up and down and cheering.

Suddenly, the loudspeaker crackled. The circus announcer's voice boomed out of every corner of the gym. "Ladies and gentlemen! Boys and girls! Without further ado, we'd like you to sit back and enjoy a dazzling, daring, death-defying performance by Normal's very own fourth- and fifth-grade classes. Please put your hands together for the fifth graders."

The fifth graders stampeded out to the centre ring, while the fourth graders waited for their introduction. "And now, please welcome the fourth-grade class, who are calling themselves the Flying Squirrels!"

The audience cheered as Molly, Pen and the rest of the fourth-grade class ran out of their hiding area and stood in the centre of the circus ring. As they'd rehearsed, the two classes stood in a circle and waved to the audience that was gathered on every side of them. Nolan, who still wasn't that great at any of the circus stunts, sneaked over and released a loud burp into the announcer's microphone.

Then the music blasted on, and everyone ran to his or her place. Penelope climbed up the ladder to the trapeze, along with Amelia and Norah and several fifth graders. Vivica was waiting for them at the top of the ladder and helped them all get harnessed in.

Meanwhile, Molly and Izzy jogged over to the tightrope. Some of their classmates went to the juggling area, Joey and a few of the other guys in their class started doing their clown act, and Raade got to roll around like a hamster inside a giant wire ball.

The crowd went wild when Penelope swung out on the trapeze bar to do her tricks. She went straight into a knee hang, then pulled herself back up and twisted into a double somersault in mid-air before landing gracefully in the net.

While the rest of the trapeze group per-formed, Molly stepped on to the tightrope. She got herself steady, then performed her cartwheel without a single wobble. Everyone cheered. After she bowed, Molly looked out into the audience and found her mum and Grandpa Quill. They both looked proud to the point of bursting. Molly searched around in the benches beside them for her brother, but didn't see him anywhere. She wondered where he'd gone after his performance.

Next, the kids who had learned how to juggle ran around the outside of the ring tossing colourful balls into the air. Two fifth graders stopped and tossed balls back and forth to each other in the air, without dropping even one! Molly clapped extra-loud, since she hadn't seen them do it before.

A few other fifth graders had figured out how to ride the unicycles, so they zipped around the ring trying not to crash into anyone. Almost half of the fourth graders – the ones who hadn't really mastered any of the circus stunts – ran around dressed as clowns. Nolan, of course, was one of the clowns.

Raade rolled around the ring inside his wire ball, chasing after Nolan. Nolan screeched and tried to escape by climbing one of the silk ropes that hung from the rafters in the gym. The whole audience gasped, then laughed, when Nolan's hands slipped off the silks and he rolled on to the floor, crashing into one of the unicycles. Both Nolan and the fifth grader leaped off the ground and took a bow.

After a few minutes, the announcer stepped

back into the ring and put his microphone up to his lips. He yelled, "Congratulations to Normal's fourth- and fifth-grade classes." He waited for the applause to die down, then said, "Dear audience, you are in for something truly special tonight. The Circus of the Dazzling Stars is ready to impress you with our high-flying adventures on the trapeze, impossible stunts by our wire team, and a group of clowns that is second to none. But first, we have an additional surprise guest for you tonight." The gym quieted, and everyone focused on the announcer. "Your town has been hiding a secret. A big secret."

Molly held her breath. Was he talking about the Quirks?

The announcer held up his hand and said, "I have a feeling none of you know that a circus legend lives here in your midst." He held open his hand and looked around, casting an air of mystery. "But she does! And tonight, Normal's very own Barbara DeVille has joined us to perform her world-famous juggling routine."

Penelope caught Molly's eye from across the ring. "Mrs DeVille?" she mouthed. Though Molly was too far away to see what her sister had said, she knew exactly what Pen was thinking. That was one of the things she loved most about being a twin.

A moment later, the Quirks' neighbour stepped out from behind a curtain in the corner of the gym. Mrs DeVille was wearing a billowy one-piece teal costume that covered her from the tips of her toes to the top of her neck. It was dripping in sparkles and sequins, and there was something stuck to the back of the suit that made it look like she had wings. The costume made Mrs DeVille look a little like an ornament someone might hang on their tree at Christmasstime. Molly hardly recognised her neighbour without her usual fussy skirt and silly stockings.

Mrs DeVille moved slowly into the ring as the fourth and fifth graders fanned out into the audience and got settled with their families on the benches again. Then everyone sat stunned as Mrs DeVille hobbled out to the centre of everything, covered in sparkles. One of the circus performers handed her several long items that looked like bowling pins. A moment later, one end of each of the pins burst into flames! All the lights in the gym went off, and a lone spotlight shone straight on Mrs DeVille.

Mrs DeVille smiled uncomfortably, stretched her arms above her head, and began to juggle. The pins flew through the air, higher and higher. Flames flashed in the darkness. Everyone screamed and cheered and clapped. Molly and Penelope couldn't

believe that this was the same woman they knew only as their spying neighbour.

As Mrs DeVille transfixed everyone in the audience, Molly's attention was captured by a tiny figure darting from the edge of the benches to the staging area. Moments later, Finn dashed out of the darkness at the edge of the gym and ran to the centre ring.

Molly gasped, but then she realised she was the only one who could see her brother. No one else seemed to notice him at all. No one could see his golden costume, or his enormous, feathered hat, or the too-big, studded cowboy boots. Finn had obviously found something fun to wear in Mrs DeVille's closet full of costumes.

Finn turned to look at Molly and stuck his tongue out. He opened his mouth wide and showed Molly that his gum was gone. Invisible, Finn was getting a few extra moments in the spotlight. Molly just shook her head and watched as her brother dashed madly around the ring.

He jogged to Mrs DeVille's side and hovered outside the spotlight. Finn reached into the pocket of his costume and plucked out four gold balls. He began to juggle. Molly watched, impressed, until she remembered that everyone could see the balls Finn was juggling. Suddenly, people began to notice that beside Mrs DeVille, a few golden balls seemed to be juggling themselves in the shadows outside the spotlight. There was a murmur in the crowd, and people pointed at the place where Finn was standing.

But before anyone could investigate or get up close for a better look, Mrs DeVille glanced to her left. When she saw the balls that seemed to be flipping around in the air beside her, Molly saw her neighbour lift her eyebrows just the tiniest bit. Finn glanced up at her. In the next moment, even though she couldn't see him, Mrs DeVille winked down at the space where Finn was standing. After a final, powerful arm toss, the two jugglers finished their routines at the exact same moment. Finn tucked the balls back in his pocket, and together Mrs DeVille and Invisible Finn took a bow.

The whole town of Normal jumped to their feet and gave a standing ovation. Then every classroom

joined Mrs DeVille and Finn in the centre of the ring. "We did it!" Penelope cried, running over to stand with her sister.

"We sure did!" Molly agreed with a huge smile plastered across her face. "We survived Mrs DeVille and her snooping, and we totally rocked at the circus."

Both girls felt a small body trying to burrow in between them as they stood with their class and took a bow. Molly glanced down and smiled at her brother in his silly circus costume. The girls separated just enough that Finn could squeeze in. As the three Quirk kids made their way to their front-row seats where they'd sit with their mum and Grandpa Quill to watch the rest of the show, Finn said, "Circus Quirkus is ready for the big time, don't you think?"

"Not quite yet," Penelope said, giggling.

"Maybe when I can juggle fire, like Mrs DeVille." Finn sighed. "Someday."

"Maybe someday," Molly agreed. "But right now, I am definitely ready to sit back and enjoy the show."

Acknowledgements

I owe thanks to many people for their support and encouragement while I was writing the second book in *The Quirks* series – and for their ongoing support of the series as a whole!

First, thanks to my husband and family. Most especially, I owe a barrelful of circus treats to my own quirky kids, who really ought to be listed as co-authors on this book. I love sitting around the dinner table every night brainstorming fun new ways for Finn to get into trouble!

Next, thanks to the team at Bloomsbury: Jennifer Edwards and Jennifer Gonzalez, who have been huge supporters (and have become great friends); my marketing and publicity crew – Beth Eller, Linette Kim, Cristina Gilbert, Bridget Hartzler, Erica Barmash, Lizzy Mason – who have juggled the launch of this series like circus pros; my brilliant editorial and design pals – Michelle Nagler, Brett Wright, Cindy Loh, Caroline Abbey, Catherine Onder, Patricia McHugh, Melissa Kavonic, Donna Mark, John Candell; cheers (and a haggis) to Polly Whybrow and my publishing team in the UK; and of course, illustrator Kelly Light: *mwah!*

As always, thanks to my agent, Michael Bourret – his job can be trickier than juggling fire.

I am extremely grateful to the incredible booksellers, teachers and students in California and Minnesota who have been extra-supportive and have made the launch of this series so fun. Special thanks go to The Wild Rumpus, The Red Balloon, Mrs Nelson's, A Great Good Place for Books, Once Upon a Time, Piragis's Second-Floor Bookstore, Burroughs Elementary, and Homecroft Elementary.

Finally, thanks to the Minnesota State Arts Board, which provided a generous Artist Initiative grant that allowed me the time to write this book without a circus of children running around me.

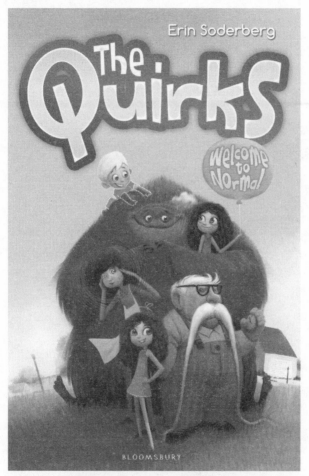